I AM RAHAB: A Novel

Part 2

by JC Miller

To: Monique
Thank you for
the support
Please review
love
JC Miller
2019

ISBN: 978-1-7339386-1-7 (Paperback)
Library of Congress Control Number: 2019911966

This is a work of fiction. Any references to historical events, real people, or real places are used fictitiously. Names, characters, and places are products of the author's imagination or used in a fictitious manner..

"Aba Daba Honeymoon" written and published by Arthur Fields and Walter Donovan in 1914. Credit: Library of Congress, Music Division.

"Bring me the sunset in a cup" by Emily Dickinson, written in 1924.

"Friend We Have in Jesus" by Joseph M. Scriven, written in 1855 and composed by Charles Crozat Converse in 1868.

Front cover Art Brittany Lewis, Yum Productions Art
Book graphic design Chanel Smith, WPD Media LLC
Editing Tiya Marshall, Marshall Editing and Consulting

Printed in the United States of America.

First printing edition 2019.

Jess, Mo' Books LLC
P.O. Bx. 1808
Albrightsville, PA. 18210
JessMoBooksLLC.Wixsite.com/jmbllc

Dedicated to Mommy, I miss you.

Table of Contents

Section Four: Soundview
Life After Death
Mrs. Jenkins
Snap Beans, No Salt

PROLOGUE

"What do you see?"
I said, "I see a boiling caldron; and it is tipping away from the
north."
Jeremiah 1:13

If it is possible to smell death, Rahab can smell it on Jeremy. The foul odor passes through his pores and ripples from his breath.

"Why, Rah? Why?" he shouts over her silent terror. But she can't speak. There's nothing to say; her words can't undo what's already been said. She's his captive, yet she's aware that she's more than a prisoner.

Jeremy's mind screams for him to surrender, raise the white flag! But prison isn't an option. Yo! Players don't go out like that. They go out HARD. His sanity debates with the sense of insanity gripping him. Rahab's trembling body held against his alerts him; it's not about the game anymore. She's involved. He releases a sigh of despair.

"I love you," he reluctantly confesses; three words he's never uttered before. He then plants a sloppy wet kiss on her forehead. "If this is it...it's gonna be you and me forever, Bonnie and Clyde style," he concludes, drawing Rahab closer as though trying to consume her. His trembling hand tightly grips the gun he is pressing against her temple.

Click. Jeremy cocks the pistol, ignoring the pleas from those in the room. His own heavy breathing is all he can hear. I always hated the way that movie ends. Remembering Bonnie and Clyde were killed in cold blood, Jeremy prefers to hold his and Rahab's destinies in his hands.

At that moment, time stands still. Rahab's family, helplessly watching the ordeal, freeze. Their stone-like faces grimace in agony. Rahab's tears stop flowing and become plastered to her face. She can't move; her body is stiff. From the corner of her eye, she looks up at

Jeremy. His eyes, frozen upon her, have lost their intensity. He doesn't look like himself, and he seems conflicted, an inner war plays on his long face. Rahab's body becomes numb as a calming peace washes over her. She closes her eyes and gives everything she has to Him, the Lord.

BANG! The gun fires.

From her mind's eye, Rahab's entire life flashes before her. She can see the little teal house on Charlotte street in the South Bronx. She can feel Minton's grip on her arm and see his cold bloodshot eyes. The smell of Crack fills her nostrils.

Am I dead?

PUAH LOVES MINTON

A HOUSE IS NOT A HOME

The soulful sound of *Luther Vandross* blares through the dimly lit basement of the three-bedroom home. A red light hangs strategically from the ceiling illuminating the space with a sensual glow. It's a Williams/Auguste party, the last on Charlotte Street, a fourteenth birthday and graduation party for Rahab.

Remembering the past, Puah and Minton cling to each other. They grope and whine to the sultry love song. Lost in time, they identify with each painful verse and hang from the notes interplaying between melodies. Each key speaks an unspoken language that only music can express. Life can sometimes imitate a love song; it keeps you dancing even when the music stops.

Minton slowly glides his rough hands up Puah's sweat-soaked back, pulling her into a hug. *Luther Vandross* cautions: *A house is not a home* when the spirit of love has moved on. An insurmountable hole pits Minton's stomach. He robbed his home of love. He dries his tears against Puah's sweet smelling hair, inhaling all of her familiar scents. He loves everything about her and wishes he could turn back the hands of time.

Puah clings to Minton tightly, aware that he's crying. Fighting the lost battle of reconciliation has mentally and physically exhausted her. She's done all she can do and was all she could be. Her heart advocates on his behalf, pleading to give him another chance. Her mind opposes, declaring enough. Puah loves Minton, but he isn't trustworthy anymore. Hopes of love and dreams of happily ever after committed suicide years ago. Love arrived too late and missed its departure. No connecting flights.

BIG CITY LIVING

Shortly after giving birth to Silas, the itch of discontentment seized Puah. She felt robbed of her youth and spent weeks crying the *baby blues*. As with Rahab, she didn't connect with Silas. She harbored maternal feelings toward him, but the anxiety of giving him the attention he needed, or failing to do so, paralyzed her. If it weren't for her aunt, Mags, coming to the rescue, Puah didn't know what she would have done. Mags offered to watch Silas more than she should have, freeing Puah of her motherly responsibilities.

Influenced by her schoolmates, Puah found solace in the nightlife. In lieu of coddling her newborn, she mingled with a more mature crowd. Thursday and Friday evenings were spent bar hopping in Harlem, sipping on cocktails and listening to bands. Still new to the city, she didn't stray far from home. Her favorite spot was her father, Richard's, nightclub, *Bayou House of Blues*. Later, she frequented the *Lenox Lounge*. They both granted a feeling of nostalgia.

The sophistication of *taking in* live music soon wore off after experiencing the raw energy of discotheques. Puah quickly transformed into a *dancing queen*. Remembering the cotillions of her youth where she was only allowed to serve punch, she came alive on the dance floor. She spread her wings, yearning to live beyond the restraints of organized existence. *Big Wilt's Small's Paradise, The Roxy, Paradise Garage, Club Zanzibar,* and *Studio 54* became her new hangouts. Intrigued by the indulgence of big city living, Puah left Silas and Minton for the pleasures of entertainment. The effects of alcohol and cocaine won back her yesteryears. Getting involved with Terry seemed the next best thing to do.

Puah met Terry, a Caucasian lesbian, in *Galaxy 21*. Terry boldly approached her on the dance floor. Gently wrapping her arms around Puah's waist from behind, she attempted to sway to her rhythm. Unable to keep up with Puah's grind, Terry stood back and watched. Puah danced lewdly around her to *Sylvester's*, "You Make Me Feel (Mighty Real)."

Terry, a bona fide Brooklyn born and raised New Yorker, was an electrician by day and deejayed in gay clubs throughout the city by night. She was years older than Puah, somewhat stout, and favored dressing in manly attire. She introduced Puah to a world full of music, dance, sex, and drugs. On her days off, she stole Puah away from nursing school and took her on long train rides exploring the city. On other days, they *laid up* getting high at Terry's Greenwich Village apartment. Terry understood Puah's way of thinking. They talked on the phone all hours of the night while Minton slept, clueless of the goings-on.

Over the course of a two-year relationship, Terry and Puah's adoration grew to the point of Puah conceiving plans to leave Minton. She had already introduced Terry to Silas, and the three were to pursue domestic felicity.

The more successful Minton became, the more he threw himself into work. Days quickly became months and months, years. He had no complaints as long as Puah and Silas were home when he arrived, there was a hot plate of food in the oven, and a cold beer in the fridge. The icing on the cake was Puah's warm body in bed.

Eventually, in spite of Minton's love affair with his achievements, he took notice of her absence. Puah wasn't there anymore, physically or mentally. People whispered in his ear about a mysterious green *Plymouth* parked a block from their building every Monday.

Instead of confronting Puah, feeling partly to blame for any waywardness, Minton intended on winning her back. When the business was young, he used to accompany her on outings. He enjoyed the limelight and parading her around town. It pumped his chest out a few inches. He knew he was all the man she needed.

No other man can contend with what I offer.

Minton began taking weekends off, interfering with *"Terry time."* Puah didn't appreciate his advances at first; nevertheless, he aggressively wooed her.

He frequently delivered roses to her new job, wanting all the men at Bronx Cedar Hospital to know her status. He bought her jewelry, designer handbags, and anything else her heart sought after. Minton's persistence, kindness, and attentiveness made it difficult for Puah to discount him. She enjoyed the attention. Not to mention, he was good-looking, charismatic, built like *Adonis*, and had more moves than *Bruce Lee*. She fought both women and men off of him in the clubs. Minton would sit back with his signature broad smile and soak up the attention. He knew Puah was no trade-in.

Regardless, Puah didn't believe she was in love with Minton and couldn't place her finger on the reason why. She didn't consider herself a lesbian. She was sexually attracted to Minton as well as other men. Terry wasn't the first woman she'd been with. Her love affair with Daphne Fontaine was partly the reason for her being in New York City. Her feelings for Daphne and Terry were different, deeper and more profound. But, no matter what her feelings were, or how she treated Minton, he wouldn't give up.

On one occasion, he surprised her in a limo and whisked her away to *Sag Harbor* for a romantic weekend getaway. Suited in a black tuxedo, he stood in front of the hospital with a dozen long-stemmed red roses in hand waiting for Puah to get off of work. Little did he know, Terry was also there waiting to steal a few moments herself. She parked behind the white stretch limo wondering about the occasion. Then she saw Minton, *dressed to the nines* and bearing gifts, exit the vehicle.

"Dang it!" Terry shouted, banging the steering wheel and accidentally honking the horn.

Startled, Minton quickly turned to survey the area. Not recognizing the white woman with the mullet haircut in the green *Plymouth,* he turned away and continued his mission of waiting in front of the glass entranceway. He repositioned himself, smoothing out his suit, patting down his afro, and making a breath check. *Green Plymouth?* Before he could add one and one together, Puah squealed. "Minton! What are you doing here?"

Puah noticed Terry parked in her usual spot as she came off of the elevator. Then Minton as she approached the doors. Nervous, Puah shrieked and jumped into his arms. She hugged and suffocated him with panicked kisses. The other nurses exiting the building sang *oohs and ahhs,* giving Minton the once over.

"What are you doing here?" Puah repeated, taking the flowers he extended toward her. Her face felt hot. She hoped not flushed.

"Surprise, bay-bee," Minton answered, smiling like *Kool-Aid Man.* "It was fifteen years ago today I met a sassy, stuck-up, colored girl who thought she was white. She kicked me in my shin, twisted my ear, and stole my heart all at the same time," he declared, holding her tightly. Puah blushed at the thought of him remembering their first encounter.

"Aww, Senior, that's so sweet." She inhaled the beautiful roses. "But! As I recall, you deserved that kick. You were a cocky little big-headed boy."

"May this big-headed boy take you away on a mini vacation?" He dramatically bowed, beckoning her toward the shiny white limo behind them. "Your chariot awaits, my queen."

Puah's mouth fell open. In her nervousness, she hadn't noticed the vehicle. Using the roses to cover her astonished and rattled face, she screamed. They hadn't traveled since moving to New York City. She was excited, yet she felt bad for standing up Terry.

Puah tried not to look in her direction, but she quickly glanced her way as she was walking toward the limo. Terry threw up her arms, gesturing *what about me?* This time, Minton did notice the obviously angry, red-faced woman. *Could Puah possibly hurt me like that again? Naw.* The thought quickly left his mind.

THE KEY TO HER HEART

In the following months, Minton seized every opportunity to plan romantic dates and Puah, a glutton for indulgences, enjoyed the attention. Terry could feel Puah slipping away and had no intention of being shoved aside. The little time they shared, Terry spent interrogating Puah about her whereabouts and goings-on with Minton.

She started showing up at the clubs Puah and Minton frequented, flaunting attractive women on her arm to make Puah jealous. She caused Minton to grow suspicious by calling the house late at night and hanging up when he answered. He grew tired of wondering and began tossing accusations.

"I hope you're not playing yourself, Pu!" he'd say. Every now and then, he'd refer to *Johnny Taylor's* song, "Jody's Got Your Girl and Gone," saying, "What's this all about? Jody better watch his back."

The stress of a love triangle caused Terry and Puah to begin arguing regularly. On a Monday evening, after parking further away from Puah's apartment than usual, they got into a falling out. Terry insisted Puah leave Minton.

"It's either him or me," she demanded, feeling entitled.

"It isn't that easy, and you know it."

Puah left the car, slamming the door before the argument turned into a fight. Terry had an Italian temper and Puah a Creole one. The combination was explosive.

Puah marched home convinced that she'd had enough of Terry's whining. Instead of going directly upstairs, she stopped by *Dirty South,* the dry cleaning business Minton owned on the ground level, seeking to question him about his long overdue marriage proposal. He wasn't there. The employee behind the counter informed her that he had just left for Albany. Minton was meeting with some owners in regard to property; he was considering a second location. Remembering he mentioned that, Puah left. She went across the street to *Church's Chicken* and ordered two spicy dinners with lots of fried okra instead of fries for later.

Terry approached Puah from behind as she fumbled with her keys. "Open the door, and I promise not to make a scene," she whispered.

Puah granted her wishes, not caring for a public display. Terry pushed past her, loudly arguing in a thick Brooklyn accent. *Fugetaboutit.* Puah begged her to lower her voice. The dogs, King and Queen, were agitated. Terry ran up the stairs threatening to confront Minton. Puah followed.

"He's not home; you should leave."

"If he's not home, open the friggin door."

"Stop, Terry, please. Shhh!" Puah shushed the dogs through the closed door. "Why are you doing this? I can't deal with it right now. I have to go pick up Si," she fibbed, knowing he was with Mags and Richard for the night.

"Open the door!" Terry insisted, encouraging the dogs to start barking again.

She knew Puah's schedule better than she knew her own. Puah opened the door against her will, worried that Minton's employees and customers could hear the screaming and barking. She would have some explaining to do later.

Once in the house, Terry forcefully pulled Puah into her arms. She squeezed her tightly, declaring her love. The dogs growled, awaiting the word to attack.

"Shhh!" Puah hissed again, beckoning them to leave. They whimpered and sat down.

Terry removed the chicken dinner bags from Puah's hands and set them aside. Proceeding to beg, she stroked Puah's face and kissed her slender neck. "I'll kill myself if you leave me," she insisted, gazing intently into Puah's eyes. Puah began to cry. "Don't cry; you know I love you. I'd do anything for you. I don't wanna make you cry," Terry assured, wiping her tears away. Then, ravishing Puah's body, she removed one item of clothing after another.

Puah loved Terry, but the relationship was becoming too much. The newness of the romance wore off a long time ago, and Puah was beginning to wonder if the excitement of an affair was all she wanted in the first place. *I'll let her down gently tomorrow.* She allowed the woman, who knew her likes and dislikes and cared enough to abide by them, to caress her longer than she should have.

Minton was on the highway to Albany when he noticed he'd forgotten his briefcase and turned back. He found the ground floor door and the apartment door open. Minton tipped up the stairs prepared to encounter intruders. He cautiously snuck into the apartment, mad at himself for not carrying his pistol. The dogs greeted him, jumping and wagging their tails. He quietly shushed them. Puah's purse and the dinners were on the table. He could hear muffled music coming from the bedroom. *Why would she leave the doors open?* He was confused until he noticed the discarded apparel littering the narrow hall.

Jody is dead.

Minton slowly turned the knob before opening the door. The background music grew louder. He slid in the room and suddenly paused, dumbfounded.

Another woman?

Blood rushed to his head. His pulse raced. Sweat drenched his forehead. Slowly, he staggered toward the bed attempting not to alarm them. He preferred the element of surprise.

How could Pu do this to me again?

The man he feared and subdued within himself surfaced like *The Hulk*. In a single agile movement, he lunged forward grabbing Puah by the throat and thrusting Terry to the floor. Alerted by the scuffle, the dogs ran into the room. Barking aggressively, they growled and nipped at Terry. Terry stayed put. She had hit her head on the wooden dresser and was confused.

Minton lifted Puah from the bed by her neck. Her feet dangled the air. She gasped and grabbed his tightened hand as her breaths shortened. Gazing down beyond his dilated pupils was the countenance of a man gone mad.

In the blinking of an eye life mingled with death, and after the initial shock passed, she knew she was in love with him. Love, in its purest form, unconditional. In that instant, she knew she always loved him.

That time when she considered suicide, butterflies fluttered in her stomach when Minton entered the room. "Hello, Pu," he said, and she thought she'd heard the voice of God. He forced death from her hands. Yes, he was her hero but more than that. When he stared into her eyes on the porch of the Fontaine Estate, licking her arm, her body awakened but her spirit leaped. He called on her when no other boy would dare bother with the Voodoo lady's daughter. She shunned him, and he kept coming. Puah found herself in their childhood laughter. There she was allowed to be *free. Free* from Mrs. Fontaine's constant grooming. *Free* from the perverted stares of the good Dr. Fontaine. *Free* from the teasing remarks of the stair step trio who often resented the attention she received. Puah cowardly detached herself from Minton's love. She was afraid she couldn't return the love he rightly deserved. The same type of love Silas and Rahab required.

Gasping for air, she considered how Daphne and Terry made her feel. With them, she disregarded the world. They listened as she rambled on, caring only for herself. Being with them was like giving the world the infamous middle finger. Loving Minton confronted her with herself. To love him was to give of self. Her soul quaked with the revelation and the anguish she'd caused her best friend.

With what little breath she could muster she apologized. She revealed her love for him and told him how she wasn't deserving of his. Minton's grip weakened with every word that poured from her lips. He thrust her down and turned, punching the concrete wall and fracturing every finger in his hand. Bellowing in pain, he hastened out of the apartment, kicking the walls and tossing objects out of his way.

"Senior wait!" Puah yelled, coughing and trampling over Terry.

Holding his arm against his chest, Minton staggered down the staircase and out of the building. Puah followed. She stepped into her undergarments, shoes, and trench coat.

"Please, allow me to drive you to the hospital," she pled, taking his keys from him. He leaned against his car door in pain. Too much pain for rational thought.

"Please, Senior," she begged, attempting to guide his noncompliant body toward the passenger side.

Minton looked at the drawing crowd and then at Puah in her short trench and heels. Her hair was tousled, and red lipstick smeared across her face. She looked like a floozy version of *Baby Jane.*

"Arrgh!" he screamed in physical and mental pain.

"Please, Senior."

Mr. Lee, an employee, finally approached them. Initially, he didn't want to pry.

"Can I help, boss? Do you need me to drive?" The older Asian man softly asked. Not bothering to wait for a response, he simply guided Minton to the passenger side of the car.

"Thanks," Minton groaned, tucking his head and getting in.

"I will take him, Miss Boss," Mr. Lee assured, holding out his hand for the keys.

Embarrassed and ashamed, Puah handed them over and stepped aside. She felt like she handed over the key to her heart.

"I love you, Senior. I love you!" she yelled, crying as they drove off.

She pulled the loose trench snug against her shivering body and watched as they disappeared around the corner. Tugging the tail of the coat over her exposed bottom, she made her way through the staring crowd. *How could I stoop so low?* She brushed past Terry, who stood in the doorway.

"Pu—"

"Please. Don't ever come back here. We're done," Puah interrupted before closing and locking the door behind her.

LOST PRIDE

Puah was sitting in the living room with the television watching her when Minton returned. The dogs were fast asleep at her feet. She was unsuccessful at not worrying when she heard the jingling of keys at the door.

Mr. Lee quickly situated Minton in a chair. He then placed the keys and a bag of prescription drugs on the table near the untouched chicken dinners.

"You okay here?" he asked, laying Minton's jacket across his leg.

"Yeah. Thanks again, Mr. Lee," Minton answered, shaking his hand awkwardly with his left hand.

Mr. Lee summoned the dogs. Puah wanted company and neglected to take them downstairs to guard the store overnight. Mr. Lee nodded salutations before leaving.

Puah sat paralyzed, unsure of Minton's temperament. His arm was cast and harnessed across his chest. She reckoned he couldn't hit her but played it safe.

Mags begged her to leave the apartment when she called crying. "There are three things of a man's ya never mess with. One is his money. Two is his pride. And three is his woman. Lawd helps the woman who messes with his money and steals his pride."

She suggested Puah come stay with her and Richard until things blew over, but Puah refused. She was ready to take whatever Minton served. So, Mags requested that she check in every hour until she felt safe.

Minton sat quietly slumped in his seat. The gray suit he wore for his meeting was wrinkled and stained. The grand smile that usually greeted her was nowhere to be found. They stared at each other, not knowing what to say nor how to feel.

For years, Minton waited to hear Puah say *I love you*. Now that she had he considered rejecting her. He watched her fidget with the decorative pillows adorning the couch. She sat with her bare feet tucked underneath her bottom. Her face was clean, her hair freshly washed, and she wore one of his long-sleeved pajama tops that were too tight for his muscular arms. Her smooth skin, the color of *Werther's Original* hard caramel candy, was radiant with a healthy glow. *She's beautiful.* He rubbed the five o'clock shadow outlining his face. *"Charm is deceitful..."* He remembered his mother teaching, *"...and beauty is vain; but a woman who fears God, she shall be praised,"* she would often say, teaching him to choose wisdom over charm.

I should probably start going back to church. I haven't done that since Mama died. Minton looked around the room. I definitely need to get rid of all of this Santeria Voodoo crap. He looked at the glass of water and green coconut placed behind the front door. What the heck is that for?

At the end of every month, Puah religiously has her cards read by Señora Martha. She returns home from every visit with some spiritually charged product or device. Once, she brought home a three-foot-tall wounded Jesus looking statue. Minton freaked out, demanding that she take it back. Being raised a devout Christian, he refused to partake in most of Puah's Voodoo antics. However, he chose not to practice his religion either.

As many people do when pressed by circumstances, Minton considered attending a church. *It's time to make a change. Ma would be disappointed in me. Maybe some common sense will rub off on Pu. That is if we make it?* He shook his head feeling overwhelmed with thoughts.

"Come here," he finally requested, sitting tall and extending his good hand.

Puah leaped from the sofa at his command. Hefty tears beat her feet to the floor. She fell to her knees apologizing.

"I love you. I swear I do. I'm selfish and stupid," she declared.

Minton wasn't sure of what to say. All he knew was that he wanted to feel her smooth skin against his. He laid his hand on top of her damp head and combed his fingers through her curly black hair. At his touch, she wept louder. He ran his hand down her neck and back around toward her face. Cupping her cheek in his palm, he wiped a tear with his thumb. Tears instantly filled his eyes after noticing the imprint of his hand bruised around her neck. He recalled how he and his mother used to lock themselves in the bathroom and care for wounds his father inflicted. Minton couldn't help but wonder if his mother had crushed his father's heart. Ashamed of his thought, he allowed his tears to fall freely upon Puah's head in a haunting cry. He wrapped his good arm around her neck and drew her near. They bawled together, both remorseful. With his nose pressed against Puah's coconut scented hair, he decided that life wasn't worth living without her.

In spite of the pain, Minton stood up, scooping his woman up into his good arm. She wrapped her legs around his waist, and he carried her down the hall. Nine months later, Elizabeth Gomer Williams was born.

A FRESH START

Puah and Minton considered the pregnancy a fresh start. Neither dealt with the underlying issues of a broken heart and mistrust. Attempting to reclaim Minton's love, Puah became docile. Minton became distant. He loved her but wasn't sure if he was *in love* with her anymore.

Determined to be the man that his father wasn't, he unintentionally became him. He threw himself into work, opening another dry-cleaning location. Eventually, pretending all was well led to drinking and using drugs.

Puah blamed herself. She chased Minton out of love and into the arms of every attractive woman feeding his ego. *I made him feel like less of a man.* The only way she knew to get Minton back was to join him in the nightlife they both enjoyed. Pretending to be a *Suzy Homemaker* wasn't working.

Misery loving company as it does, Minton showed no opposition in Puah rejoining the fantasy world of drugs and alcohol. It made him happy to dance with her in his arms and to drink until they stumbled home. Her hanging out was subtle at first, but knowing women were after her man while she mothered their children changed the game. Before long, it was back to *living for the weekend* and sleeping off hangovers. Mags and Richard acquired two weekend grandbabies.

Minton did reclaim his love for Puah but not without repercussions. Whenever he felt suspicious, he grew jealous and angry with rage. The first time he hit Puah, it took them both by surprise. She received a gold herringbone necklace for that. The *first punch,* a fur coat. The *first broken tooth,* diamond earrings. The first time he hit Silas for mouthing off while defending his mother, he ended up taking them all to Disney World. A drug-induced beast slowly grew within Minton, robbing him of self. There were good and bad days until Rahab came, then every day was bad.

Eventually, he lost everything. To make matters worse, Puah was fired after thirteen years of service with Bronx Cedar Hospital for suspicion of stealing medication.

Although Puah loves Minton, her life and the lives of their children depend on her leaving him.

GOODBYES

Luther Vandross repeats *a house is not a home* as the heart-wrenching love song comes to an end. Being in Minton's arms is everything Puah desires, but better judgment tells her, *love doesn't pay the bills. This house isn't a home.*

Minton looks physically stronger, better than he's looked in a long time. He was away at a drug clinic for nearly three months and now wants a fresh start at their relationship. Puah fiddles with the thought of reconsidering their breakup, but she's tired of being dragged around.

She stiffens her body against the rhythm of the love song. If they continue like this, her body just might get its way.

Stop holding on to the past. It's time to move on.

She takes a step back from her coaxing partner. Minton gently tugs at her arm, but Puah shakes her head no. Her feet are firmly rooted in severing their relationship. He exhales deeply, unconsciously releasing a lifetime with her, then turns to make his way past their dancing guests to the staircase. If he's lucky, she'll follow. Puah hasn't yet told the kids that they lost the house and, in Minton's mind, that's a sign of her reluctance to leave him. She and the kids are supposedly moving in with Mags and Richard in a few days.

If they do, I won't be joining them. There's about as much going on in that house as it is in ours.

In January, Richard suffered a stroke. His health has been rapidly declining ever since and, because of that, Mags hasn't stopped drinking. It's September.

Minton excuses himself past a group of kids gathered in the stairwell.

I'll smoke a stogie and wait for Pu in the bedroom. If she doesn't come up, I'll say my goodbyes and leave.

RAHAB AND LYDIA

A FRIENDSHIP FOR PAIN

In true Williams/Auguste family fashion, Rahab's birthday/graduation celebration has turned into an adult affair. Cramped along the basement stairwell, Rahab, along with a few friends and her younger brother, Silas, are fooling around and laughing at the grown-ups grinding two-step. The party, to Rahab, so far is just alright. She's been anxiously waiting for her *crush*, Jayson Simmons, to arrive and make things one hundred percent better. The only reason she agreed to the celebration was for the opportunity to be with the hazel-eyed, cinnamon toast colored *homeboy*. Jayson or Jay-Skii Money, as the kids respectfully call him, verbalizes in street slang. He woos the girls around the block with his hip persona and *fresh gear*. Rahab spent the entire summer secretly admiring him from afar. The only person who knows of her crush and everything else about her is her new best friend, Lydia.

Lydia and Rahab met two years ago at Sacred Hearts Catholic School during detention. The first ten minutes of detention, the girls sat quietly afraid. The next ten minutes, they whimpered and sniffled, realizing how much trouble they were going to be in. For the last ten minutes, they held hands crying loudly. Neither uttered a word. They intuitively knew they shared the same fate and fears.

Rahab, as well as Lydia, had a horrible first day of Junior High. Lydia, who assumed the title of awkward, always had trouble making friends, but on that particular day, a group of girls picked a fight with her and only she was found at fault. Rahab wasn't in the mood for being teased that day either. In spite of her neatly groomed appearance, the kids made fun of her swift speaking Creole accent and discarded her as being weird. Having had a bad start that morning, Rahab entered in an altercation with the first person to insult her.

The bad day started early that morning with Minton *laying down the law* as they rode into school. It was the first time the two were alone since she arrived in the city. Right away he proved he wasn't the romantic hero Puah painted on the train ride to New York from Louisiana.

"I want you up and ready to go when I'm ready!" he yelled as Rahab settled into his vehicle. She was three minutes late. "If you do as I say and stay out of my way, we may get along. I don't tolerate back-talk or laziness. You do your share, and we'll be okay," Minton clarified as they drove along the route to Sacred Hearts. "Don't ever think you're better than my kids because you're not. They get first dibs; you don't. That's just the way it is. We didn't ask for this; this is you and ya mama's mess." He continued to yell while parking the car in an unutilized lot.

Where are we? Rahab knew it wasn't school property but refused to ask Minton. She was boiling mad at him. Then, she remembered how Dr. Chester had fondled her near the secluded lake back in Louisiana. *Why are we here?* She looked at Minton. He sat quietly trying to gather his thoughts. Minton looked back at her. She was flushed and puffed with anger. The countenance of disgust crept upon his face. Rahab reminded him of John Jr. raping Puah. *How dare this little byproduct sit here annoyed with me.* He was getting angrier by the second.

"Listen here, you crumb snatcher; I love Pu, but so help me, I'll kill her if she ever leaves me," he threatened, feeling the beginnings of a mutiny. "If I ever find out that you are saying or doing anything to pull us apart, I'll kill you, too. That's a promise," he said, using the word *kill* as though he'd done it before. Rahab swallowed hard.

"You're nothing to me but a seed that should've wasted." Spit strayed from Minton's mouth as he yelled and speckled the side of Rahab's face. Enraged, he punched the dashboard.

Rahab was afraid. Her heart raced, but she fought back the tears that threatened to fall. *If he touches me, I'll scream.* She remembered what her friend, Salmone, taught her about a woman's rights. *Why does he hate me?*

"This is our new spot, me and you, and if you ever tell about our spot so help me..." Minton paused briefly and physically turned Rahab's face toward him. "...I thought of killing your father once, but your grandmother convinced me not to. She's not here to stop me from killing you. Don't test me," he warned, pointing an erect finger in her face. She looked smug, so he forcefully mushed her forehead, banging her head against the car window.

Before she could cry or scream, Minton shifted out of park and quickly reversed out of the vandalized lot, managing to avoid oncoming traffic. Rahab's heart leaped from her chest. She didn't know what to think. All she knew was, *never anger Minton. 'Out of the frying pan and into the fire' is what Big Mama would say.*

Gazing up at the cloudy gray sky that seemed to engulf her existence like a snow globe, a tear escaped her eye. She remembers Pastor Josh's prayer during their phone conversation the night before.

"May God bless you and keep you," he said. "And the peace of God, which surpasses all understanding, may it guard your heart and your thoughts in Christ Jesus."

Where is this God that is supposed to keep me? Rahab sighed. Where is my peace?

Minton drove four blocks without speaking a word. He double parked in front of the school that Puah insisted that Rahab attend because of the local junior high's high pregnancy rating. Minton smiled and spoke kindly to passersby. He had an image to upkeep. Everyone knew him and returned warm salutations. Like a gentleman, he opened Rahab's door. She hesitated to get out.

Minton sighed then bent and whispered with a smile on his face, "Second warning. Don't test me. I suggest you get out of this van."

AWAITED FATE

Rahab and Lydia, knowing their awaited fate, slowly walked down the drab corridors together after detention. They introduced themselves and agreed to be friends.

"I know I'm getting beat with da chancla," Lydia, a pretty Latina, revealed as she nervously bit her already too short nails.

She was awkward indeed. Her orange stained *Mercurochrome* elbows and knees stole attention from her face, but if you took the time to look past her shield, you'd discover a head full of curly black hair, deep-set brown eyes, and thick eyelashes that batted in innocence. To Rahab, she seemed afraid of much more than her mother's slipper.

"Ah don know what's gonna happen to me," Rahab added, feeling uncertain like a prisoner on death row. "But ah knows I'm dead."

"Where jú from?" Lydia asked, scrunching her face as she noticed Rahab's accent. She was fully aware of her own over exaggerated one.

Lydia had a gift, the gift of avoidance. When she was nervous or didn't want to be bothered, she mimicked her mother's thick broken Spanglish accent. Other times, she claimed not to *speakah da English* at all. She hadn't quite figured Rahab out, but she knew she was different like her.

"Louisiana," Rahab answered. She beamed proudly remembering the better part of her life. "You from here?"

"Sí, yes. Mi familia is from Puerto Rico, but I was born here," Lydia answered taking Rahab's hand as they approached the exit doors. "My name is Lydia Maria Cruz. You can call me Le-Le."

"Okay, ah will, Le-Le," Rahab responded smiling, pleased to have made a friend. "My name is Ray-hab Ah-gu-stay," she slowly emphasized. "Ah goes by Rah."

"Rah! I like dat name. It's a good name. Like rah, rah, when you cheer for something good. ¡Hurra!" Lydia shouted, holding Rahab's hand in the air.

"Rah, rah, rah!" they yelled, to the nun's shushing.

Quickly, Lydia and Rahab became fonder friends than she and her best friend from home, Salmone. Their friendship would surpass memories of childhood pleasures, the awkwardness of teenage wonder years, and the arduous journey to young adulthood. They clung to each other like a favorite blanket, needing the comfort of a good friend. It was a gift from God. Both girls were subject to abusive stepfathers, and their mothers were emotionally detached.

"What makes a woman want to stay with someone who beats her?" They often discussed their mothers' predicaments, both declaring neither would fall prone to that type of relationship. The answers they received from their mothers were usually compiled of complicated mixed emotions ranging from hurt to emptiness. No matter the response, the *commas* separating each excuse were the children.

Rahab and Lydia were both tormented in one way or the other by their labeled stepfathers. The corrupt men, sharing in malice, addictions, lack of moral integrity, and judgment ruled over their subjects with executed anguish. Lydia was violently beaten and sexually molested. Her mother, out of desperation for stability and love, played deaf, dumb, and blind to her daughter's plight. The torment never reached penetration, but the acts were so vile that Lydia knew actual intercourse was next. On two separate occasions, her stepfather attempted to have relations with her.

The first time, instead of driving Lydia to school, he took her to a grungy motel. She looked so pathetic, pleading and sobbing in emotional distress, that he took what he called *pity* upon her. They ended up doing the usual sickening acts that he enjoyed.

The second trip to the motel another woman was involved. This time, Lydia's stepfather forced her to perform with the woman while he watched. He found the prostitute to be more intriguing, and she ended up taking Lydia's place in bed that day. However, not without a warning that her turn was coming. He said he was spending too much money on what was rightfully his for free.

In an attempt to keep her stepfather and other predators at bay, Lydia stopped bathing. She acquired an odor which gave the kids at school something else to tease her about. On several occasions the school called Lydia's home threatening to report her parents to child welfare services. Lydia's mother lied, stating that they had a plumbing issue. When she approached her daughter Lydia used the opportunity to confess the truth about the stepfather. Her mother insisted that she was lying, but Lydia knew that she was aware of what was going on and it made the abuse even harder to bear.

One morning, when the stepfather was dropping Lydia off at school, the Vice Principal, Sister O'Connor, came out to meet them. With her back as straight as a board and her glasses resting on the tip of her narrowed nose, she stood by the curb waiting for Lydia's stepfather to roll down the fogged window.

"La bendición," the stepfather nervously said, greeting her with respect and a blessing. He didn't know what else to say.

After clearing her throat, Sister O'Connor told him of Lydia's demerits due to uncleanliness and asked if he was aware of the calls and mail sent to their home. Sister O'Connor informed him that Lydia was one infraction away from being expelled.

"This matter is inexcusable, unsanitary, and neglectful on your behalf," she declared. She then went on to demand that other means be found for Lydia's daily personal hygiene.

Sister O'Connor humiliated the stepfather in a harsh yet eloquent manner. Lydia had never seen so many shades of red appear on a face at once. That day the proverbial shoe was placed on the stepfather's other foot, and it didn't fit him well.

"Do I make myself clear?" Sister O'Connor asked, erecting her bent back. Her traditional *habit* blew against the March breeze like a *she-ro's cape.*

"Yes, Sister," the stepfather whispered.

"Excuse me; I didn't hear you, Mr. Colon," she said, placing her hand behind her ear.

"Yes, thank you, Sister!" he repeated, nodding several times.

Lydia chuckled inwardly and entertained thoughts of becoming a nun.

That night, the stepfather beat Lydia and her mother with an iron's detachable cord. He spewed colorful words in both English and Spanish, describing how disgusting and wretched they both were to him. Then, he forced Lydia to undress in front of him and her mother. He openly observed her curves before running a tub of hot water and dragging and dumping her in it.

Lydia screamed as he harshly scrubbed her body with bleach. Her mother cried and pled, but he was angry and unobliging. He was mad at the nun and mad at the *estupidos*, as he called Lydia and her mother. To him, they were as dumb as door knobs.

"Year after year you fail me," he shouted, pushing Lydia's mother away, but she ignored his claims and steadily attempted to unclog the drain. With each attempt came a lick from him.

"Mi bebe, ay dios mio! Mi bebe," Lydia's mother cried.

"Cállate!" Lydia's stepfather ordered, punching her mother in the face. She tumbled backward, hitting her head against the white tiled wall.

Quickly wiping the blood from her nose, she scrambled back to her knees. Cupping her hands together she begged. "Stop! Papi, por favor. Don't hurt her, please. I'll do anything. Papi, no!"

The stepfather suddenly stopped. He slowly turned facing her. He was both amused and angered by her plea. *What can she do for me*? An awkward silence fell upon the small, crowded bathroom.

"What can you possibly do for me... Huh? You're useless. You're both useless," he shouted before dunking Lydia's head under the water.

Lydia fought violently, splashing hot bleached water everywhere, but he held her head firmly against the bottom of the old porcelain enameled tub.

"Nothing, that's what! You and your stupid daughter can do nothing for me." Lydia's mother pulled his arms, begging him to free her drowning child. "Estupido!" The short olive-complexioned Latino shouted, releasing Lydia's head. She emerged, coughing and gulping for air. Her face reddened as she gagged and puked into the tub. Lydia's mother wrapped her scalded body in towels, and they cried in an embrace.

Disgusted, the stepfather slapped them both across their heads with the wet washcloth he held.

"Stupids. You deserve each other. You are both officially dead to me," he declared, pushing past them to exit the bathroom.

"Ay, Papi, no don't say that," Lydia's mother responded, grabbing him by the arm.

"All you want is my money. You don't love me. All you think about is that retard." He gestured toward Lydia who stood frozen with fear.

"Ven acá, don't leave," her mother continued begging.

Fed up with her moaning, the stepfather violently shoved her face with the palm of his hand, knocking her into Lydia's arms. Lydia held her mother tightly, although she fought to be released. They watched as the stepfather stormed away. He usually stayed away for months on end, but when Lydia figured him gone for good, he reappeared, jiggling his car key in her face.

***

Rahab's situation was different but just as evil and immoral as Lydia's. Minton placed her in uncomfortable situations where she witnessed drug use and sexual behaviors.

Every morning before school, Minton parked the van in *their spot*. Then, he climbed over the bench seats into the service compartment and snorted lines of cocaine. In the beginning, having some pride left in himself, Minton didn't bring drugs into the house. He dreaded the thought of his kids, especially Silas, discovering the truth about him. Rahab, on the other hand, was another story. What she thought of him was irrelevant. Minton wanted her to feel his pain. He blamed her for everything wrong with Puah and wanted her to pay for being born. From the back of the van, Minton hurled insults at Rahab and blew lines of coke.

As time passed, Rahab didn't mind those days. The days when Minton was content with belittling her and getting *nice* before work. That was before his habits changed. Eventually, he welcomed prostitutes into the back of the van where they *blew coke, shot up*, and paid Minton with sexual favors.

As Minton's addiction worsened, so did his attitude toward Rahab. Threatening to take her virginity, he kept her in constant fear. Rahab would sit in the front of the van panicked with thoughts of Dr. Chester running through her mind while trying not to listen to the familiar moans coming from the back compartment of Minton's van.

"If ya mama don't start acting right, you'll be taking her place. Ain't nothing in this life free. Take notes," Minton threatened, laughing.

Rahab recalled her Big Mama, Lotti, uttering those words as she preached over the sound of water boiling and the flapping of hanging sheets. *"Ain't nothing in life free, beb."*

The possibility of having to repay Minton for his hospitality kept Rahab anxious that first year of junior high. Her grades suffered until Minton caught wind of them. From then on, every marking period, all the kids in his house were summoned to line up in front of him with their report cards in hand. If anyone, except

Gomer, the little princess, received a grade under 'B' they were beaten on the spot with a thick leather belt.

WHITE LINES

When Silas started Sacred Hearts Catholic School, Rahab's situation with Minton slightly changed. Minton still parked in the lot, but now that Silas was with them, he and Rahab were told to walk the remaining blocks to school. Minton was no longer a *functional user*. His rendezvous with pushers, users, and prostitutes couldn't wait.

Minton sold his first dry cleaning location to his employee, Mr. Lee, for a portion of its worth. Living his lifestyle and running two businesses was showing up in his work. Mr. Lee convinced Minton to sell before he got too far in debt. Instead of working to strengthen the other location he owned, Minton blew more money on drugs.

Minton and Puah hosted and frequented elaborate parties. They owned and bought even more fancy *things*. They treated their children like trophies on a shelf, dusting them off every so often for appearances. Minton showed off Silas, calling him the handsome, handy work of his loins. He bragged about how the girls were already lining up. Puah did the same. She pranced her daughters around in matching Gordon Gartrell outfits with faces shining of *Vaseline*. She made Rahab come out during their parties to show their guests how well she danced. The guests enjoyed the entertainment and laughed in merriment, all the while Minton *snorted life up his nose* and *shot dreams down his veins.*

Afterwhile, Minton began selling drugs. More of a user than a seller, he ultimately fell into debt with dealers who supplied his product. Eventually, he took a second mortgage out on their home to pay off the dealers and managed to keep his body parts attached, but it didn't deter him from using. He went back into debt and lost the second cleaning location, and, finally, their home.

FOREVER CHANGED

"Is this what y'all did last year?" Silas questioned Rahab, dumbfounded by Minton's anxious behavior and his dropping them off in a vacant lot.

"Yeah," Rahab lied, gazing straight ahead. She held Minton's secrets out of fear for her life. She once told Puah that Minton threatened to kill her and Puah brushed her off.

"That's all talk. Senior's pulling your leg," Puah insisted. Minton's temper was hot, and Puah knew it, she just hoped that he wouldn't harm Rahab. Puah was aware of Minton's extensive drug use, having discovered *tracks* on his arms and legs but she still fronted him money and stole meds from work for him. He would always say he loved her and provided excuses about the depth of his addiction.

"What does he do there?" Silas continued questioning Rahab as she walked swiftly away from the vacant lot. "What about our hot school breakfast? Isn't that why we left the house early in the first place? What's so important?" Rahab had never made it to school for breakfast, and on several occasions, she missed first and second-period classes as well. It all depended on Minton's drug of choice and the woman of the day.

Unable to withstand the suspense, Silas doubled back to the lot. He had to see for himself what the *obvious* secret was.

"Si wait!" Rahab yelled, following and begging him to turn around. The more she begged, the more suspicious he grew.

They briskly journeyed back through the urban community, crawling that time of the morning with prostitutes, drug dealers, and Cross Bronx Expressway traffic.

Silas' disappointment in his father traced his face and appeared through his saddened eyes. When he peeked through the window of the van, he saw Minton with another man. He'd never witnessed anything more heartbreaking. The visual was too much information for a twelve-year-old son to partake of dear ol' dad. He instantly lost respect for Minton and no longer viewed him as a man. *My father's a sell-out.*

The sight caused him to strip Minton of medals of admiration. "This can't be Senior," Silas mumbled to himself.

Rahab felt obligated to explain. She felt she somehow betrayed or let Silas down. So, she told him what Minton often told the pushers when he was *short* with their money.

"He's sick, Si. And confused dat's all. Dis isn't him, it's de drugs. Let's not judge, okay?"

Silas didn't respond to her. He was done with the topic and done with his father.

The children never discussed what they saw that day. They both pretended to put it behind them, but Silas was forever changed. He fell in line with the daily routine as Minton continued to drive them to the lot every morning and they walked to school from there.

Chance had run its course for Minton. The victory of success and the likelihood of prosperity made way to *male prostitution.* The strong ruggedly handsome Louisiana native reduced himself to *payments* for drugs, a fate far from the goals he had once set for himself. He was reluctant at first, but after a while he *bent over* to the strongholds of addiction.

THE LOT

As torturous as school days were, the restless evenings while Puah worked were worse. Rahab, Silas, and Gomer barely slept. Minton stayed up all night coming down off drugs, high on drugs, or needing more drugs. He was also destructive, slamming and breaking things. Puah had to hide what little the family had left at Mags and Richard's house to keep him from selling or breaking everything they owned.

On Puah's nights off, she would calm the beast. She and Minton locked themselves in their bedroom and didn't come out until daybreak. After years of housing pleasure, the bedroom had become Puah's prison. Inside the darkened room, she soothingly reminded Minton of who he used to be and, throughout the night, he wept for his lost soul. The kids trained themselves to sleep through those moan-filled evenings, but the nights of disorderly bluster usually ended in physical violence. No one knew when their turn was coming, and anything was likely to trigger Minton's temper.

Once, somewhere around two in the morning, Minton emptied a bag of garbage over Silas' head as he slept in bed. "Make this the last time you forget to take it out!" Minton yelled at the top of his lungs. He then forced Silas to get up to go throw the garbage out into dumpsters around the corner from the house. Silas was angry, but he complied; if he didn't, somehow Rahab would *pay the price.* Frustrated, he stormed out of the house wearing only his tee shirt and underwear. The next morning, he ended up staying home sick, and it was back to business as usual between Rahab and Minton.

They shared dirty looks the entire ride to the lot. Minton made Rahab sick to her stomach. He wasn't the dictating tyrant anymore. He was a sloppy and raving mad addict, and Rahab couldn't tolerate him any longer. Before Minton could come to a full stop, she had already retrieved her bookbag and began to push open the door. Minton quickly grasped her arms, feeling a bit of repulsion himself that day. In a heartless manner he announced, "Nah, I think we're staying here today." He played with the thought of taking Rahab's innocence. He wanted to rape her of everything she had. *I lost everything!* But he harbored no desires toward her although she was developing into a beautiful young woman with a body of someone twice her age.

"But ah have school. I'll be late," Rahab quickly interjected, attempting to squirm her arm from Minton's grasp. "You don't want truancy to start calling de house again, do ya?" she reminded him, feeling proud to finally have the upperhand.

Minton ignored her. "Climb over," was all that he said as he removed the key from the ignition.

Their eyes fixed, and Rahab's heart stopped. Minton's solemn face, sunken and edgy from drugs, read caution. In being pretentious, she'd forgotten his threats regarding her virginity. As she dropped her bookbag on the floor, she thought of fighting him. She contemplated her odds of winning but realized he wasn't high yet, so she did as she was told.

Rahab could hear Minton exiting the van and relocking the doors behind him as she climbed over the seat. Empty hanging garment bags once filled with neatly steamed clothing awaiting delivery fell freely in front of her like a plastic shield. Rahab cowered in a corner. She could hear Minton speaking with someone. A female. *Thank goodness.* She breathes a sigh of relief remembering the burly man that she and Silas witnessed him with earlier that school year. The compartment doors swing open. Minton enters first followed by a frail young white woman dressed in skimpy attire. The woman was twenty-two, but she looked well into her thirties. Living the *street life* had done away with her beauty. She depended on Minton for shelter, and he depended on her for drugs. Rahab slumped into the corner where she hid hoping Minton would forget she was there. She quietly watched as he cautiously brushed the young lady's hair behind her ear. She sported a black and blue eye that Minton tenderly kissed. To Rahab, Minton seemed to care for the mysterious woman. For a second, he resembled the man he used to be and not the *junkie* he'd become. The young lady removed drug paraphernalia from her purse followed by two small bags of heroin. Minton began to bounce around like a kid in a candy store.

They prepared their drugs in silence, intently focused on the task at hand. Only a few grunts and a light slap in frustration were shared between them. Minton swiftly removed the dry-cleaning uniform that he still wore every work day even though he'd lost the businesses. At this stage in his addiction, there was no rhyme to his reasoning. Without shame nor ill intent, he pulled down his underwear and the young girl tied off his private part with a shoestring. She then proceeded cautiously to insert a needle into a healthy vein.

"Don't bunk up, Sam!" Minton yelled, nervous yet eager.

"Shhh," she urged, pulling the plunger slowly, just a tiny bit, to see if blood came through.

Minton patted her head like she was a *good dog* and leaned against the van wall. "I knew I kept you around for a reason," he slurred.

"Wait for me," she laughed, quickly tying off her arm.

Rahab was afraid to breathe. She was positive she could get a *contact high* from the lingering non-ventilated odor coming from the drugs. The two *addicts* didn't seem to be bothered by the strong smell. They muttered a few grunts toward each other before zoning into a heroin-induced trance. Rahab sat in the corner afraid to move for what seemed like forever. She watched as they leaned back and forward, and from side to side without tipping over. She wasn't sure if they were nodding off or slowly dying. When she finally ushered the nerve to move, Minton lunged forward, grabbing her arm.

"Where you going, Pu, huh?"

"It's me, Senior, Rah."

"Stop lying! You going to meet ya girlfriend, aren't you?" he insisted, backing Rahab against the locked swinging doors. "What's her name? Who is it this time?" Minton pressed his body against Rahab and raised her chin toward his face. "Do you love her more than me? Would you leave me for her?" he asked softly while attempting to crush her skull between his large hands.

"Minton, it's me," Rahab declared, slurring through squished cheeks. She was terrified.

Suddenly, Sam the prostitute began to laugh. "Here I am, baby. I'm that trick you looking for," she said, whining her hips in a clumsy vulgar manner.

Minton swiftly turned and grabbed Sam by the neck, thrusting her into a corner where she fell, pulling the empty plastic garment bags down with her. In a delusional rage, Minton beat her like she was a man, ignoring her pleas. Frantic, Rahab gathered her courage. With as much haste as she could muster, she climbed the bench seat, grabbed her backpack, and escaped through the driver's door. She could hear Minton yelling behind her.

"Get back here, Pu! I'm not done with you yet!"

Rahab quickly turned to see if he was chasing her. He stood in the distance, *buck naked,* yelling obscenities in the middle of the street. She ran. The sensation of the cool morning air burnt her lungs. She escaped unforeseen doom yet again.

Minton returned home three days later. He looked sick and wore a hospital ID bracelet. As usual, he didn't mention anything about what happened between him and Rahab. She doubted he remembered. For the remainder of the school year, she and Silas walked from the lot.

THE VIRGINITY PACT

In the midst of their troubled lives, Rahab and Lydia considered each other a sister. If Lydia wasn't hiding at Rahab's house, Rahab was hiding at hers. A refuge was hard to find, but stolen moments were treasured amongst them.

In spite of the abuse, they were normal 80s girls. They watched *ABC Afterschool Specials* while doing homework. They talked like *valley girls* and fantasized over celebrity crushes. They purchased *Word Up, Tiger Beat*, and *Right On* magazines for the posters, and giggled on the phone for hours. As close as Rahab and Lydia were, Lydia never replaced Salmone.

Out of all the people Rahab spoke of, common or celebrity, Salmone topped them all. To Lydia, he became a star. She admired how Rahab's eyes sparkled when she spoke of his heroism. Rahab lost herself in remembering his companionship. Lydia wasn't jealous. She lit candles for Salmone during mass. He was important to Rahab although his memory grew painful over time.

The bayou buddies grew distant in communication. Weekly phone calls turned into monthly calls, then holiday and special occasion calls mostly from the adults. Rahab used to write, but Salmone's return letters were so far and few between, she eventually stopped. Their conversations became unpleasant. She lied about being happy in the city. She feared he wouldn't understand. His father, Pastor Josh, would *alert the authorities* as he threatened to do in the past. *Child Welfare Services* would separate her from her siblings and Puah, then throw them into foster care as Minton informed. Salmone and Rahab's short and awkward conversations eventually turned into yelled hellos from the background of family chats. Lydia was indeed a pleasant addition to Rahab's life.

The summer of Rahab's fourteenth birthday, she and Lydia orchestrated a plan to elude the raincloud the stepfathers held over their heads. The doting friends often spoke of running away, marrying their heartthrobs, and living happily ever afterlives. That was a normal conversation for them. But the humdrum summer of '84 was different. Instead of discussing plans for marriage, careers, and how many children they intended to have, they made immediate plans to lose their virginity before their stepfathers stole it from them. Both girls agreed it should be with someone they liked. Rahab chose Jayson Simmons while Lydia chose Silas.

Rahab couldn't imagine why her friend was committed to *crushing on* her brother. It was awkward. Lydia was almost a year older, and she saw how badly he treated the girls that threw themselves at him. Rahab didn't want Lydia to get hurt, or worse, lose their friendship over her brother. Silas was hardly innocent. Puah couldn't keep girls off of him with a bat anymore; she needed an entire baseball team.

Silas hung with the wrong crowd and skipped school. He doubled back to their neighborhood in the mornings, leaving Rahab behind. He smoked weed and Rahab was almost positive he sold it, too. However, Lydia found him enchanting. Whenever he was around, she stared, so much so that he felt awkward and would leave. Lydia marveled at how his thick curly black hair stood neatly piled in a *high-top fade* and never wavered from its style. She loved how his eyes slanted like a lion's and curled when he smiled, giving him a *chinky* look. Her heart raced whenever he entered the same room as her. It nearly jumped out of her chest when he teased her and called her the nicknames he made up just for her. He'd ask, "How's it going, Bucky Le-Le?" or "What's up, Bugs?" while tousling her hair. She adored the nicknames, although they mocked her overbite and large front teeth. The fourteen-year-old girls, too young to make decisions concerning their bodies but tired of having no authority over them, composed a plan. Taking a *blood sister's* oath, they promised to have sex with their crushes the night of Rahab's graduation party.

SEVEN MINUTES OF HEAVEN

When Jayson finally arrived, the teens made a *beeline* to Rahab and Gomer's room. They planned their own *red-light* party, equipped with spiked punch, chips, and music.

Before entering the room, Jayson stops Rahab in the hall to apologize for being late. He promised Silas he would attend the party even though he never officially met Rahab. He only knew of her. All the guys around the block *knew of her. They all* felt she was "*hot to def*," but she wouldn't give them the time of day.

"Sorry, I'm late. I was helping my brother set up for a block party in Harlem. He's a DJ. You probably heard of him, Buggy Love?" Jayson yells over the loud music coming from the basement. "A House Is Not a Home" has been answered by *Tina Turner's* "What's Love Got to Do with It."

"Uh, yeah. Ah tink so?" Rahab lies, feeling nervous. She can feel beads of sweat forming on her nose.

"My brother said I can spit some rhymes tonight, maybe even spin a few records. So...I'm gonna cut out early. I hope you don't mind," the *flyy guy* explains, taking Rahab's hand. She nearly loses her mind. "I was hoping...maybe you can come watch me. My brother's parties are fresh...not that yours isn't."

Rahab exhales deeply, lightly tapping her sweaty nose. "Nah ah...ah can't. Pu, dat's my moms, she'd freak out," Rahab stutters, trying to sound cool but a Creole accent is difficult to elude.

"You're cute," Jayson voices, smiling. He brushes his finger across her cheek and acknowledges the boys watching with a *wassup* nod.

The teenage posse sits, listening to Jayson's mixtapes. They bop their heads, sipping punch and eating chips, each pretending not to feel awkward in their skin. After some time, Lydia, sticking to her blood sister oath, suggests that they play *Seven Minutes of Heaven*. A game where two people of the opposite sex are sent away for seven minutes of heaven in a closet or bathroom. The three girls and three guys sit in a circle on the floor and spin a soda bottle to see who would pair up. Rahab spins first, and the bottle lands on Silas.

"Ewww!" everyone yells in disgust, agreeing to a respin.

Tookie and Javier are chosen. Everyone *oohs* as they slip away into one of the two closets in Rahab's room. Once they're gone, Lydia suggests that she pair off with Silas. "...because any other combination is just nas-tee."

Silas agrees with the mastermind. He secretly harbors an identical liking for the short, shapely Puerto Rican girl with cute buck teeth and *Bambi's* eyes. He leads Lydia to his room. Rahab and Jayson are left alone.

"I guess it's you and me," Jayson informs as if she doesn't already know. He awkwardly cracks his knuckles and clears his throat.

Jayson Simmons, the finest boy on the block is in my bedroom. Rahab attempts to hide her excitement.

"Nice room," he compliments. "I see you like *New Edition.*"

"Yup." Her eyes dot across the walls from poster to poster of *Ralph Tresvant,* the lead singer from *New Edition,* her celebrity crush. His perfectly captured smile enchants her. Suddenly Rahab feels as though she's cheating. *Is this the end?* Then her eyes lock with Jayson's. *He's sooo cute.*

At that moment, reality supersedes fantasy, and teenage dreams fade along with printed smiles on posters. *Sorry, Ralph. I can't wait on you forever, but I'm still lost in love.*

"So...you wanna stay out here or should we go in the closet?" Jayson asks, now leaning on his elbows stretched comfortably across the floor.

"Ah guess de closet," Rahab answers, believing she's ready to become a woman.

Butterflies flutter in her belly. She has more than *making out* in mind and hopes he does, too. She's unaware that, in spite of his cool demeanor, fresh nicknames, and hip 80s gear, Jayson's also a virgin.

The nervous teens head to the closet, sweaty palm in sweaty palm. Jayson leads the way; although inexperienced with what she has in mind, he's a pro at closets. Once inside, Rahab stands against the door and locks it behind her back. Jayson extends a hand above her head and the other in his pocket.

"What you wanna do, shorty?" he asks, sticking to his *hip front*.

Wanting to get *it* all over with, Rahab wraps her arms around his neck and engages him in her first kiss. Instantly, Salmone comes to mind. Inwardly she's always believed they would be together. Even when boys weren't an inkling in her mind, she knew Salmone would be there.

Now, he's somewhere thinking about other girls.

Her clumsy first kiss turns into the real deal and thoughts of childhood acquaintances vanish in the tenderness of Jayson's lips. Rahab's fears of what happened at sunset by the lake with Dr. Chester temporarily vacate and a new outlook on intimacy is created.

"What's going on in here?" Minton yells, bombarding the room. He has a hunch from the looks on their guilty faces.

Rahab and Jayson are exiting the closet. Jayson, standing taller than he did walking in, and a smug Rahab, pulling him along. Tookie and Javier, who were waiting patiently, snicker as they get up and leave.

Minton's dotting eyes survey the scene. *What has she done?*

The couple spent longer than the usual *seven minutes of heaven* exploring and, although *the expedition* wasn't as Rahab dreamt, she appreciates her choice pick. Jayson gently tucked her hair back into place and made sure she was tidy before opening the closet. Feeling a desire to keep her around he nervously whispered, "Rah, will you be my girl?" He encouraged her response with a peck on the cheek.

"Ah already am," Rahab replied, feeling sassy. She winked and took his hand, leading him out of the closet.

"I said, what's going on?" Minton repeats, locking eyes with Rahab. Her stare is cold, and he senses an air of arrogance.

Unexpectedly, the sting of accountability stabs his heart.

What have I done?

He submits to her stare down by lowering his head. He's been drug-free for nearly three months, and in his sobriety, he sees her as she is; *just a kid.* Puah's kid, and his responsibility. Rahab's never mattered to him until now.

Ashamed, Minton redirects his attention toward Jayson. He looks conflicted like he wants to make a run for it, but his newly claimed girl has his *nose wide open.*

"Lil' homie, excuse yourself," Minton conveys in a calm tone Rahab hasn't heard before.

"Me?" Jayson nervously asks, pointing to himself. He glances between Minton and Rahab. Their eyes are fixed on each other, and the room is full of tension. "Oh, okay. I'm sorry."

He leans to kiss Rahab goodbye but notices Minton moving in. Familiar with Minton's intimidation tactics and feeling rebellious, Rahab throws her arms around Jayson's neck and kisses him.

Touché. Minton remembers the countless times he's placed her in uncomfortable situations. He sighs deeply, feeling the uneasiness of having to watch a public display of affection. He rubs his itching hands over his head. Then, tucks them deep into his pockets, attempting not to explode as he's prone to doing.

No longer able to stand the *PDA*, he clears his throat, then yells, "Okay, enough!"

Jayson takes Rahab's hands and gently sway her arms back and forth like Minton isn't there. "You sure I can't change your mind about coming to watch me deejay?" He coyly bites his lower lip.

"Bye, homie!" Minton yells assertively before Rahab can answer. He steps aside and gestures Jayson toward the door.

"Aiight," Jayson responds, raising his voice, a tad bit annoyed by the neighborhood druggie. "I'll catch you later, shorty," he says to Rahab and arrogantly walks backward toward the door staring at Minton. Jayson palms his groin in a *hoodish* manner of *chutzpah* and gestures an upward nod toward Minton accompanied by a twisted mouth and exits the room. Rahab smiles pleased with him but Minton puffs up in anger. Feeling the backlash of disrespect played out toward him, he heads out to follow Jayson, but Rahab intervenes.

"Whatever you do, you can't hurt me no more," she declares. Her eyes fixated so deeply on him she can see his soul. A wave of courage sweeps over her. "You can't take from me what ah already done gave away. You can try, but you'll never be my first. Ah gave dat privilege to someone ah chose," she defiantly informs him, digging her finger into her chest attempting to hold back tears. "It was mine to give or take to begin with. Naw you, or no one else can steal dat from me."

"Rah, please," Minton appeals, interrupting the now crying girl. He moves in closer inclined to console her. Rahab steps out of his reach.

"No, don't touch me. Don't ever touch me again!" She shouts, willing to fight. The spirit of her Big Mama, Charlotte Auguste, rises in her tiny body. She positions herself, feeling like *Muhammad Ali.* She reckons she now knows of the pleasures of relations and the ecstasy of young love; she'd rather feel the coldness of a moist grave than to be forced upon by any man.

"I'm sorry...I would have never done that to you." Minton struggles to explain, choked with emotions. He's been selfish and angry for far too long, murdering spirits in the process. "Never! I know I'm a monster...but I would have never done that to you. I just...I mean...I was trying..." he continues, failing in communication. Sorrow paints his once handsome face. There's too much to say, and he can't find a way to explain. "I'm sorry." He quickly exits the room before his tears fall.

Rahab weeps, angry with herself for feeling pity toward him. She wants to be mad. In the two years they've lived together, she's never seen him remotely resemble a human being. Even when he was manipulating others with his charming demeanor, she could always read straight through his act. This time he seemed sincere, and that's throwing a wrench in her program. She feels like running after him, but she can hear her Big Mama's voice. *"De only ting more pathetic den a broken heart is a foolish heart. It's made of putty."*

It's true; Minton hated Rahab. He blamed her for every downfall cast upon him. Coaxing her into fear charged him like the witch who replenished her youth through *Rapunzel's* golden locks. Abusing Rahab and his family rid him of frustrations but, inwardly, he never wanted to hurt anyone.

She's just a child.

Minton scurries out of the door of their home on Charlotte Street. The summer evening is settling into nightfall; the street lights softly illuminate the tree-lined neighborhood. Tears of anguish line his face, not for himself, but for those he's hurt. "She's a baby!" He allows the truth about Rahab to resonate in his spirit. He considers turning back to beg for her forgiveness and maybe even convince her to take another path in life, one not bent on revenge and destruction. *Who am I? Who will listen to me? I'm a washed-up druggie who hardly recognizes himself in the mirror. What good is a loser to a family who's better off starting over without him? The best thing is for them to forget I ever existed.*

Minton wipes his tears and lifts his stiff collar high enough to hide his face. Tilting his *Kangol* over his eyes, he turns the corner off of Charlotte Street in search of his final fix. A desire to relinquish his life waves over him. He sobs violently, hating the man he's become. The *weight of life* presses upon his shoulders, but his disappointment in himself outweighs worry. *God, is this my punishment?* He questions, slipping into a darkened back alley.

"*Pride always comes before the fall,*" he can hear his mother saying of his father's foolish pride. Minton pauses and leans his hot back against the coolness of a brick building to compose himself. He never intended on becoming like his father. He decides, rapping a secret code onto a steel door. *I won't be returning. I'd rather die than watch Silas become like me. One last fix and then it'll all be over.* He enters a room filled with certain doom. *Goodbye, Puah Marie, my friend, my lover. I wish our journey was different, better for you than I. I pray that life will treat you with kindness. As for me, c'est la vie. I've found joy knowing we were love.*

STRIVERS' ROW, HARLEM

HEAVEN AND HELL IS ON EARTH

Don't be afraid of those who kill the body, but are not able to kill the soul. Rather, fear him who is able to destroy both soul and body in hell. Matthew 10:28

"Are you sure, Le-Le?" Rahab concerningly questions. Lydia's face wears fear and worry, and there's a loneliness in her eyes that Rahab hasn't seen before.

Lydia allowed her secret to pass her lips and drift into the ears of her best friend. Now the words freely bounce from wall to wall as though searching for a continuation of the sentence, an *and* or a *but.* Neither girl knows what to say. They stand face to face cramping a small bathroom stall in a trendy Manhattan loft. The hook to "Heaven and Hell is on Earth" by *20th Century Steel Band* that Jayson's sampling over mixed records vibrates through the thick oak restroom door and confirms Lydia's sadness. *Good and bad go together.* She and Rahab retreated from the Christmas party Jayson's deejaying to have a moment alone. It's been months since they've seen each other and, although an inappropriate place for earth-shattering news, Lydia couldn't wait any longer.

With their backs slouched against a tagged-up stall wall, the reality of playing with fire burns an impression upon their wonder years. Lydia hasn't seen her period in three months, and the suspicion of pregnancy is seeping in.

"I don't know what to do. What am I going to do?" Lydia cries.

"Ah guess first we should find out if you really pregnant or not. Maybe take one of dem home tests," Rahab relates, trying to assist her weeping friend. "Or, what about de free clinic Pu took me to for birth control pills? Dey do er'rything der, and it's private." She rubs Lydia's back and inwardly creates a mental note to start taking her contraceptive pills regularly.

What are we going to do? Rahab squeezes Lydia tighter. *What if she's pregnant - then what?* Memories of scared young girls seeking freedom from abortions by Big Mama haunts her thoughts. She closes her eyes and tries to shake off the images. *Ain't no blood relation of mine being pulled out and thrown in no bucket, that's for sure.*

The girls, so focused on getting away from their stepfathers, didn't plan a pregnancy. They simply wanted control over their bodies. Foolishly, they chose to believe that *M.A.S.H.*, the future prediction pen and paper game they used to play regularly, gave an accurate read on their future. Everything was all mapped out until *real life* stepped in.

SI AND BUCKY LE-LE

When the Williams family moved from their home on Charlotte Street, Lydia thought she would die. The move was so sudden and abrupt. There was barely time to think, let alone react. One moment they were celebrating Rahab's graduation and birthday, the next they were moving. Suddenly, for Lydia, there was no friend to ride home with from school. There was no one to take her side when the world condemned her. No friend to share life with and no place to hide from her stepfather.

Then there was Silas. Determined to choose to give up her virginity, as opposed to the stepfather taking it, Lydia gifted Silas the night of Rahab's party.

She entered his room, dimly lit and disheveled with tossed clothing and sneakers. Silas sat on the edge of his unmade bed and pulled out a joint from beneath his pillow. He *lit and puffed* while watching Lydia undress. There was no need for awkward small talk.

She danced for him like the women from the stepfather's videos. Silas played it cool; he didn't say a word, but in his mind, he wondered what was going on. He couldn't believe his sister's friend was acting so eager. Lydia approached him like a predator seeking prey, and he briefly thought of Rahab.

What is she doing with Jayson? Was this all planned? He knew the besties did everything together.

Silas knew Rahab liked Jayson. She begged him to bring him to her party. The smooth-talking *homeboy* was popular with girls, and it seemed he could have any of them he wanted. The rumor was, he had. Silas believed Rahab could handle herself, but he thought of going to check on her. He didn't want his sister to become a notch on Jayson's belt. But Lydia. She finally got her hands into Silas' dense curls causing his head to roll back and began nibbling his neck. Altogether, he forgot about Rahab and Jayson's belt.

"Oww! Yo, chill, Bugs!" Silas yelled, squinting and wincing in pain.

"Sa-vee," Lydia expressed through her Spanglish accent, becoming nervous. She folded her arms across her chest, embarrassed.

Silas leaned back on his elbows and took a few short puffs of his joint. He inhaled the pungent smoke then released a thick, gray, skunk smelling cloud in Lydia's face. She sucked her teeth.

"Staa-pid, stoo-pid!" she whined, waving the smoke from the air.

"You need to chill," he stated, releasing more smoke alongside his grunted words. He could tell Lydia was disheartened by her snappy retort. He *hit* the joint again. This time he quickly sat up and grabbed the back of Lydia's neck and *shotgunned* smoke into her mouth. She instantly choked, and Silas laughed.

"Chill with it, Bucky Le-Le. Breathe it in like air," he ordered, passing Lydia the joint.

She paused for a second, having never smoked pot before, but she wanted to be with Silas. She wanted him to be her first. *This joint may not be such a bad idea.*

The floor dropped from beneath them and the blue walls decorated with pictures of women from the *Jet Magazine Beauty of the Week* segment began to spin. The evening was colored in reds and blues, and greens all blending into a unified hue. The color of sweat. Lydia became the woman from the hotel room, confident in herself. She floated over the colors grasping for freedom and the will to love and be loved. She became everything she thought she wasn't and more. She was beautiful, smart, and with Silas. When she awakened the next morning from the pot-induced experience, she was naked with her back pressed against his.

"Whoa, this is a pleasant surprise!" Silas expressed, turning around to face her. They had both passed out.

Lydia was frozen in confusion. Her wide eyes glued to the blue painted wall in front of her. Upon hearing his voice, she thought, *I'm stuck in a dream.* Then realized she was very much awake. His hairy leg swept across hers. Lydia panicked, flopping over on her back. She couldn't recall the day, time, nor her location.

"Easy, Bucky, you're still here with me. At my house." Silas pushes his fingers through her thick intertwining coils, pulling them upward through his fingers. *She's beautiful.*

Her eyes, brown and full, held innocence, fear, and kindness. He always thought she was cute, even when she stared at him like a stalker. "You stayed the night, remember?" He playfully peeked under the sheets.

She remembered. Her mother had given her permission to stay. She and Rahab planned it that way. They wanted to stay up all night talking about their newly found womanhood and laughing over outwitting the stepfathers. Lydia couldn't remember anything past locking Silas' door. *Am I a woman now?*

She pulled the sheets under her chin. Then she remembered spinning, floating, grasping, and trying to take hold of herself. *What was in that joint?*

"I can't remember anything," she confusingly muttered.

"I can help you remember," Silas playfully responded, tickling her.

"Stop, stupid." Lydia giggled girlishly, pretending his lightweight body was too cumbersome to push away. *He's so cute!*

She studied his thick eyebrows dancing above the frame of his perfectly shaped nose and admired how his hair still stood tall and hoped hers was somewhat decent. Smiling, Lydia threw her arms around his neck, not knowing when or if she would ever have another opportunity like this. He kissed her, and suddenly she recalled how the reds and blues and greens made her feel, and she kissed him back.

Then, they moved away from Charlotte Street. Everything Lydia was, became everything she wasn't again. She was held back in the eighth grade and all alone at Sacred Hearts Catholic School. She was picked on by the girls, tortured by the boys, and invisible to teachers and staff.

As lonely as school was, she felt more alone at home. Her mother worked late and hung-out even later in efforts to forget Lydia's stepfather. He had disappeared again. To make matters worse, she was also pregnant and rent and tuition were overdue.

It would seem that with the number of problems that Lydia had, longing for Silas wouldn't have been an issue. Instead, every night she dreamt of him. If there were a way to bottle the air he breathed, she would have. Fearing she was possibly pregnant scared her but being rejected by him scared her more.

Lydia had hopes that Silas would return to Sacred Hearts and they'd build a relationship, but he didn't. Puah registered him into a school in Harlem. Lydia heard that he stopped attending and that he returned to the old neighborhood every morning to catch up with his mischievous friends. He didn't bother to make arrangements to see Lydia, and that hurt her deeply.

VERY SPECIAL

In spite of the current situation, Lydia and Rahab manage to have a decent time at the Christmas party. The likely pregnancy weighs on their hearts, dampening spurts of laughter and hindering complete enjoyment. Lydia's smile is fake. Her moves are stiff, and her company is dry. Eventually, she complains of a headache and sits behind Jayson at the DJ booth.

Rahab and Jayson have been inseparable since her birthday party. Around the way, they're called the Black *Romeo and Juliet*. The *Stacy Lattisaw* and *Johnny Gill* of the hood - *a perfect combination.*

The last few gigs Jayson assisted his brother on were so successful he booked four parties himself. Rahab attended each one. At first, she stood in the background passing him records. Because she was a huge hip-hop fan, holding up the wall was hard for her to do, but she was intimidated by the crowd. Jayson took notice of her intensified and well-kept to the beat head nod and encouraged her to take the dance floor.

"Go ahead, do ya thang," he eagerly suggested. But Rahab was too shy. So, he familiarized her with her beauty and bestowed upon her confidence through compliments. Slowly, she began to step away from her shadow.

Now, when Jayson feeds the turntable *booty shaking beats*, Rahab inhabits the dance floor as though rehearsed. She mesmerizes the crowd - blocking out the world around her.

"The spirit of Zydeco is in your bones," Puah declares.

All Rahab knows is that music momentarily grants her freedom through movements that defy the acts of normal dance. She can *Break Dance, Smurf, Poplock, Beenie Weenie, Cabbage Patch, Fila, Pee-Wee,* and any other dance with the best of them, but it's her spirit that's captivating. Her moves aren't tantalizing, for she's not fully aware of her sensuality. They're simply alluring.

Jayson is confident to *move the crowd* with Rahab backing him up. When he plays "Planet Rock" by *Afrika Bambaataa and the Soulsonic Force,* everyone knows she's taking the floor. The beat provokes the reserved Creole beauty to lose total control.

The party crowd isn't the only circle they managed to impress. Both Rahab and Jayson earned placement into *LaGuardia High School of Music & Art and Performing Arts* music and dance programs before they even started dating. Puah urged Rahab to audition for the specialized public school, having big dreams for her talented daughter. She wanted her to experience *Fame* she never gave herself a chance to achieve. Rahab's raw audition was so engaging that, before she left the building, she was guaranteed admission as an incoming freshman.

After five hours of pounding music and pretending to have fun, the only thought Lydia can retain is leaving the party. The girls arranged for a sleepover and the anxiety of seeing Silas after three long months is setting in. All Lydia wants is to hear him reassure her. Just when she thinks she can't withstand another drum beat or scratch of a record, Jayson announces the last song.

He ends every gig with a slow jam. In a smooth, well-practiced disc jockey voice, he states, "This one is for the ladies. So, homies hold that cutie real tight. You might just get lucky tonight. If you do, thank me later. Because Jay-Skii Money is *Audi 5000!* I just dropped the bomb on this mutha tonight. Peace!"

He gently releases a record, allowing the vinyl to spin freely on the turntable. A softened melodious chime of cymbals and an angelic vocal riff began to play. Before pairing-off on the dance floor, the crowd hoots, whistles, and claps, recognizing Jayson for a job well done. He quickly removes his headset, anxious to get on the floor himself.

"Yo, shorty!" He yells toward Lydia, who's popped up and ready to go. "Do you mind crating the albums? I wanna go scoop this cutie up."

Lydia gestures him away not feeling compelled to compete with loud music but willing to do whatever it takes to leave.

"Thanks." Jayson jumps down from the platform, taking Rahab into his arms.

Debra Laws' "Very Special" is the song of choice. The teenaged couple slow dance and fantasize as they lip-synch the duet to one another. They don't entirely understand nor believe the romantic lyrics. They merely appreciate their youth, and lust for one another.

Lydia stops fussing over the records, trying to match each album with its correct jacket and watches the couples tenderly dancing, some groping, lost in their worlds. She isn't at all jealous, just admiring the possibilities. The song speaks of *love that's meant to be,* and suddenly, Lydia senses an overwhelming feeling of loneliness. She attempts to avoid crying amongst strangers by refocusing her attention on the records. Her greatest fear at the moment is that her love for Silas isn't reciprocated. *After all, for the past three months even liking me hasn't moved him to call.*

Rahab, sensitive to her friend's feelings and loyal to her brother, tries to sugarcoat Silas' behavior. She reveals that he hasn't been the same since Minton left. The truth is, the knowledge of his father being somewhere *turned out* by the streets affected him more than he's willing to admit. On school days, when Silas returns to Charlotte Street and the abandoned lot, he hopes that he'll stumble upon Minton. The man he once dreamt of becoming, as strong as *Lou Ferrigno* and smart as *Einstein,* left him feeling hollow inside. So, Silas dismissed himself from the realities of life and became a *pothead.*

Everyone was affected differently by Minton's departure. Sleepless nights and long perplexing days commissioned Puah on a manhunt as well. She checked rehabilitation centers, hospitals, and even the local drug holes, but to no avail. It was as if Minton vanished from the face of the earth. She often wondered if he died alone and with no one to identify his homeless body. Death not even he deserved.

MAGS AND RICHARD

When Jayson and the girls arrive back uptown from the party Puah is racing out of the front door struggling to carry Gomer who is wrapped in a fuzzy red *Strawberry Shortcake* blanket. She rushed home from work, heeding Silas' urging to take Gomer to the hospital. She'd been sluggish all day, but when she began feverishly talking out of her head, Silas felt it necessary to call his mother. Puah, learning they were home alone, left her client. She slipped him a sleeping pill and hoped the effects would hold until she returned.

"Does anyone own a watch around here?" Puah questions the giddy and lackadaisical teens approaching as she assists Gomer into a cab.

They abruptly end their joyous buffoonery sensing the seriousness of her tone. Since Charlotte Street, Puah's traded in her usual laid-back demeanor. Nowadays she's geared toward getting their lives back in order. The convenience of depending on Mags and Richard isn't at her disposal anymore.

The helpful hands, deep pockets, and watchful eyes of her aunt are occupied by Richard. Having suffered a stroke earlier in the year, Richard quickly developed signs of dementia. Eventually, he was diagnosed with *Alzheimer's*. Mags, hellbent on spending all of their waking moments together and all of their money on the best doctors, renowned therapists, expensive medicines, nutritionists, and 24-hour nursing care, sold their nightclub.

"Nothing but the best for my Richard," she insisted, knowing his failing condition and champagne tastes. She'd rather he dies having lived life to the fullest than live in luxury without him. "He'd do it for me. Heck, he's done it for me." She recalled her expensive stays in *Bellevue Hospital*.

It's now Puah's sole responsibility to accommodate herself and her children. After being let go from Bronx Cedar Hospital, she had a horrible time finding work in her field. Every hospital application she submitted was rejected as if she were blacklisted. After looking for work a little over four months, she finally found a sleepover position as a home health aide. She arrives home early in the morning leaving just enough time to kiss the kids goodbye before they scurry out the door to school. Before heading to bed, she briefly sits and sips coffee with Mags while entertaining Richard's demented attempts to pick her up. She gently rejects his invitations to "leave this dump for a nightcap at his place across town."

"Sorry, you're not my type. I kinda like men who aren't my father," she replies, gently rubbing his wavy, thin, silver hair backward and kissing him on the forehead.

Now and then, he'll find the strength to grab her by the waist and plop her down in his lap. She'll laugh and attempt to escape his tight grip.

"How many dollars will it take to make ya holla?"

Mags and Puah both agree that it isn't a good idea to leave Richard home alone with the girls. Mags ensured that even his nurses are men. When Richard forgets his whereabouts, he's hard to contain. Mags is the only one who can talk him down, which is why she felt comfortable that night taking him to their bar's Christmas party. Amongst old friends, Mags figured she'd have more than enough help managing him. She hoped that he might even remember them all.

Mags dolled Richard up, dying his hair and dressing him in one of his fancy creamed colored suits. They then spun off in their 1984 white on white *Cadillac Fleetwood Brougham.*

THE ATOMIC BOMB

"You mean to tell me not one of you can tell time?" Puah asks, adding sarcasm to her interrogation.

She knew Rahab was attending a party with Lydia and that they planned a sleepover afterward. She even agreed that they were deserving of much-needed *girl time,* but she didn't co-sign on them keeping adult hours. Her thoughts lean toward reprimanding Rahab, but she doesn't have the time nor the heart to grasp the steadily growing rebellious teen by the horns.

Rahab and Silas are responsible for Gomer's care while Puah works and, usually, they're both at home before Puah gets in. They have a sibling arrangement and take turns hanging out. Silas thought he was going to have an easy night of sister-sitting. Rahab informed him that Lydia was spending the night. So, he agreed to stay home with Gomer, relax, watch a few movies on *WHT,* smoke weed, play some *Nintendo Duck Hunt,* and eat pizza until they got there. The last thing he wanted was to call Puah and get his sister in trouble. They had a good system going.

"What's wrong with Go-Go?" Rahab genuinely questions, feeling a little guilty for staying out too long.

"Don't worry about how she feels," Puah responds, getting into the cab. "You weren't here when I needed you. Now, I got this!" she continues, waving an erected pointer finger and rolling her neck and eyes. "Go in the house and enjoy the rest of your little visit. Because I can guarantee, this will be the last one for a long time coming."

"Pu, I—" Rahab tries to explain.

"Nuh-uh. Pu, nothing. In the house!" She directs and demands. "And, Jayson..."

"Ma'am?" Jayson nervously answers.

"Not tonight. If momma ain't happy, ain't nobody happy. Ya heard?" She continues to snap, rolling her neck. "Go home, son. Don't your mother ever worry?"

"Yes, ma'am. I'm sorry, it was my fault."

"Nuh-uh, Rah knows her curfew. I don't wanna hear that. I gotta go." She closes the cab door then quickly rolls down the window as the *Three Musketeers* walk away with their heads low. "Don't forget to lock the door. No one leaves the house, and y'all rude behinds didn't even speak to Mr. Jenkins!"

"Hello, Mr. Jenkins," they reply in unison to Puah's cab driver friend.

For the past six months, Puah has been soliciting free rides from Mr. Jenkins. Showing a little cleavage *(here)* or a mini-skirt with crossed legs *(there)*, and *every* ride is free of charge. It's a wonder he makes any money at all being constantly on call for Puah. In the midst of flirting, Mr. Jenkins became a close friend and confidant. He helped move them from Charlotte Street. He even helped get their Christmas gifts out of layaway. More importantly, he's talked Puah off of many ledges.

"Good night, kids," the kind older man answers, peering through the window and tipping his cap. He knows each one by name.

"Go on in the house and behave. Go home, Jayson!" Puah yells, rolling up the window and sucking her teeth. She's aware that he will probably not go straight home. "Grown behind kids. They too fast," she complains as Mr. Jenkins pulls away.

"Well, we all done our share, that's for sure," he laughingly responds.

It's no secret to Puah that her older kids are *active*. As soon as they started *smelling themselves*, she took them both to the free clinic. Silas got a value pack box of condoms and Rahab birth control pills. As a nurse, Puah has always communicated with her kids regarding their bodies. She's appreciative that they're open with her in return, but she can't help but feel responsible for how active they are. *It isn't normal.* Even Gomer exhibits advanced curiosity.

Back in Puah's day, people were usually more discreet about the matter. It wasn't the topic of conversation in the home until someone turned up pregnant. Rahab told Puah she had sex the morning after it occurred. She didn't express it in the manner in which she'd planned, but she did get it off of her chest. For Puah, that bit of information was *the straw that broke the camel's back*. What little mothering skills she felt she had officially diminished. The days of innocence could not be regained.

"Pu, I'm going to the store. We're out of milk!" Rahab yelled from the outside of her mother's locked bedroom door. She was annoyed.

When Puah discovered Minton left the party without saying as much as a goodbye, she selfishly ended the celebration and retreated to her bedroom. The finality of their failed relationship shook her. She knew it was over, *but now what?* She needed to think so she ordered everyone to leave.

Rahab wanted to discuss what happened with Jayson. She wanted to express how she felt about him and even entertained telling her mother why she did it in the first place, but once more, Puah managed to shut herself off from communication.

Words of anger erupted from Rahab's mouth. "Oh, and by de way ah had sex last night right o'va ya head," she informed through the closed door, rolling her neck as her mother would do. "You were downstairs de whole time whining on ya pathetic excuse of a man at my *so-called* party, not caring about anyone else but you and him, as usual," Rahab continued in an ill-mannered tone of voice, tired of feeling like she took care of herself.

It was *as if* an atomic bomb dropped from nowhere and landed smack dab in the middle of Puah's bed. Instantly, her tears of self-pity ceased. She put out the reefer she was smoking, collected herself, and rose from the bombing, leaving her deceased spirit, dismembered from the attack, in bed. *What would Mama think of me now?* Opening her bedroom door, she saw Rahab had the audacity to remain standing there. Puah brushed past her, giving her the evil eye forcing her to step aside. She then proceeded to walk through the house as though a first-time visitor.

Puah stopped and studied the many memories trapped under glass, hanging gallery style on the walls. Smiling, she recollected each as though yesterday and deemed they were due to an updated family photo. *Gomer's front teeth are in now and look at Rah,* who stood sideways against Puah's arm in the portrait, *she looks like an afterthought.* Puah glanced over at her eldest child, still standing by her bedroom door, rolled her eyes and continued her tour. *I'm a lousy mother.* Running her red painted nails across the white walls, she gazed at the little furniture they had left and remembered when it was a fully decorated house. Heading into the living room, she pretended not to notice Lydia tipping out of Silas' bedroom. She kept focused on her journey. Puah wanted to remember everything as it was.

Satisfied, she decided it was time to make an announcement. She stood in the middle of the living room floor and screamed at the top of her lungs, "Everybody, get out! If you're not here to help me, you damn sure ain't gonna hurt me," she added, grabbing everyone's attention. They moved from their designated areas and gravitated toward her. They were afraid she was experiencing a nervous breakdown.

"We have to move," Puah revealed calmly, gazing upon each of their innocent faces. She felt disappointed in herself. "We're being put out. We don't have a home anymore," she expressed, choking up.

Starting with Rahab, including Lydia, they enclosed her.

A BASEMENT HIGH

Standing at the curb, the teenagers watch as Puah's cab disappears out of sight. Then, as teenagers do regardless of a situation, they erupt into hysterical laughing before single-filing into the house.

"Yo, Pu was off the hook. What happened to Go-Go?" Jayson asks, giving Silas a quick homeboy handshake.

Silas responds, pulling Lydia, who's acting shy and standoffish, through the doorway. "Yo, Go-Go started talking crazy and freaking out on me," he explains, openly embracing Lydia in a long warm hug. "She was saying Senior's a ghost and he's in the house talking to her. She was sweating, having chills, and vomiting. I couldn't take it anymore. I had to call Pu," he states, feeling guilty. "Sorry, Rah; I didn't know what else to do."

"Ah understand. Ah would have done de same." She tussles Silas' curls reassuring him of her forgiveness. Still wrapped in an embrace with Lydia, he plants his chin on top of her head and gently sways her from side to side. "Poor, Go-Go, ah hope she feels better," Rahab adds, then pulls Jayson along. She knows Lydia needs time alone with Silas before anyone else arrives home.

"That's some real *Poltergeist* stuff," Jayson jokes, following Rahab's lead to the staircase.

"Word! I know who Pu will be visiting tomorrow," Silas contributes. They laugh knowing a visit with Señora Martha is in order. "She'll probably perform an exorcism on Go." He looks down at Lydia for laughter. Her face is planted in his chest. *What's up with her?*

"We're gonna leave you guys alone to talk," Rahab interrupts. "Let us know when Tante Maw-Maw and Paw-Paw get in, ya hear?" she asks, beginning the climb to her third-floor bedroom.

"Yeah, aight," Silas answers, feeling a bit of tension in the air. He hopes Lydia isn't going to act funny. *She's the one who came on to me. I didn't ask for this*. Now, feeling a bit annoyed, the only commitment on his mind is the commitment to his joint in the basement.

Lydia quickly wipes her face not wanting her tears to scare him. She looks up smiling. *He's already alarmed*. She watches the vein on his temple throb. Silas leans in and nibbles her ear. He lost a *high* attending to Gomer. He's determined on turning Lydia's mood around.

"Si, we have to tawk," Lydia finally speaks, pretending to reject his advances.

"Okay, we can talk but let's do it in the basement. I was just about to go workout. You see these bullets ya boy's getting?" He flexes his arm muscles.

"Something like dat," she answers, laughing at the lanky boy in front of her.

Silas sucks his teeth, grabbing her playfully by the shoulders and gently walks her toward the basement stairs.

How do you tell a boy, who you've only slept with once...or twice that you think you're pregnant? Lydia wonders as he directs her down the steps. She feels nauseous. She's dreamt of becoming the mother of his children but not this soon. *We barely know each other.*

Silas turns on his *boombox* blasting a *DJ Red Alert* mixed tape as loud as he can. Lydia feels like she's back at the loft again. When he walks over to the casement window to crack it open so he can smoke his weed, she seizes the opportunity to turn the music down.

"I know what you wanna talk about and I'm sorry," Silas declares, attempting to beat her to the punch. He pulls her by the loop of her *Jordache* jeans to the weight bench where he's sitting.

"Saa-vee about what?" Lydia asks with a slight attitude.

"You know. I should have called," Silas answers with his head tilted like a puppy. "I should have come by. I know."

"Yeah, you should have. That would have been nice," Lydia answers, remembering her loneliness. He slowly unzips her jeans.

"Silas, seriously. We gotta tawk!" She slaps his hands.

Silas laughs, pulling her tightly against him and pointing to his puckered lips. She smirks and allows him to kiss her words away. He doesn't feel up to entertaining female drama. He longs for the attention she gave him once before. His roaming hands erase her thoughts, and before long, she's doing exactly what got her into trouble in the first place.

I'll tell him after I visit the clinic.

RED IS DEATH

Rahab and Jayson startle at the sound of a room door slamming. Jumping from her bed, they scramble for their tossed clothing.

"What happened to that warning you asked for, shortie?" Jayson whispers, hopping into his straight legged, forest green *Lees and* slipping his feet into *shell toe Adidas.* Accustomed to the escape routine, he quickly kisses her goodbye and promises to see her over the Christmas break. "I have a gift for you," he reveals, throwing a black, fur hooded, pleated leather bomber out of the window. He then pulls a green and black *Lumberjack* over his head and adjusts his rope chain.

"What is it?" Rahab asks excitedly, jumping up and down as she slips into her nightgown.

"Where is everybody?" They hear someone questioning from the stairway.

"You'll see," Jayson whispers, kissing her again before climbing through the opened window.

He wraps his legs and arms around a sturdy, winding tree growing against the house from the backyard. Once on the ground, Jayson waves letting her know he's okay before sneaking away from the gated brownstone.

"Pu!" the voice yells. Rahab closes the window, shuts the lights and heads for bed, pushing her tossed clothing underneath with her foot.

"Pu, where you at?"

It's Paw-Paw, Rahab realizes, wondering why she doesn't hear Mags or the nurse behind him. His footsteps seem to be approaching her door. Her curiosity gets the best of her; she turns on the rose-colored pillar *Fenton* lamp sitting on the nightstand and sits up. The door opens.

"There you are, Pu," Richard sings merrily, walking into the room and lightly closing the door behind him.

Amongst the boisterous and crowded bar, full of Christmas cheer, he managed to slip away from Mags unnoticed. A local cabbie, an old friend, saw him walking the streets. He picked him up and brought him home.

"Paw-Paw, it's me, Rah," Rahab clarifies, tossing off her sheets.

"I caught the red-eye all the way from New York to Baton Rouge just to see you," Richard continues, removing his jacket and tie and flinging them on a nearby chair.

Rahab climbs from the bed and heads toward him. "Where is Tante Mags, Paw-Paw? You ain't alone is ya?" Concerned, she takes his hand to lead him out of the room.

"Don't worry about Mags and me!" He shouts stern-faced. "She's so in love; she can't tell her head from her tail," he laughs, his breath smelling of the champagne toast Mags allowed him to have.

He forces Rahab tautly against his body and dances her around the room, humming an old jazz tune imprisoned in his mind.

"Paw-Paw, you hurting me! Tante Maw—" she begins to scream, but Richard covers her mouth.

"We can do this nice and easy or the hard way. Either way, it's gonna happen." He pushes her toward the bed. "I've flown too far and waited too long."

Rahab attempts to loosen her arms held behind her back, but she can't, he's too strong. She screams when he briefly releases her mouth to undo his zipper, and he clumsily covers her entire face with his large hand and forces himself upon her. Before she can think, she's being raped by her grandfather.

Richard feels twenty-five again, and everything under the hood works as intended. He moans in pleasure until he collapses over his granddaughter's limp body. He emits a howl of satisfaction. Panting heavily, he closes his eyes to collect himself. His vision blurs. His heart races. Rahab doesn't move an inch; she can't she's in shock. Her mind rejects what her heart relates for sanity's sake. They both hear the click of a *.44 Magnum* echo through the silence of the room.

Richard quickly opens his eyes, feeling the steel tap against his temple.

"Mags!" he yells, coming to himself after a year of cloudiness. "What you doing, crazy woman? I done told you about pulling guns on me," he states, cutting his eyes toward her.

"And I done told you 'bout messing with my girls," Mags counterclaims, gesturing down toward their paralyzed granddaughter.

Alarmed and confused, Richard slowly backs away from Rahab. Breathing slowly, he holds his arms up in surrender. He doesn't remember how he got into the bedroom or the identity of the young girl he pulled himself from.

"I can't explain," he sincerely cries. "What's happening, Mags?"

"I can't forgive you this time. This is my blood!" Mags pushes the gun harder against the side of his head. "Our blood! You, bastard!"

"What did I do? Please don't shoot." He cuts his eye toward the shaking gun laid against his temple and then again at the girl on the bed.

Rahab pushes herself up, aware that her grandfather is in and out of his deranged state. Although he violated her, she doesn't want him dead. She slowly turns around. Feeling both embarrassed and disgusted, she reveals her identity.

"No!" Richard yells, seeing her for the first time and realizing his actions. "My baby," he cries from the pit of his soul. *The only one who looks like me.*

Deeming he'll never be able to endure the knowledge of this great sin, and tired of living with the debilitating disease, he quickly removes the revolver from Mags' hand and shoots himself in the head.

"Aba, daba, daba, daba, daba, daba, dab,"

Said the Chimpie to the Monk.

"Baba, daba, daba, daba, daba, daba, dab,"

Said the Monkey to the Chimp...

Rahab begins to repeat the lyrics to her favorite childhood song in an effort to occupy her mind, but all she can hear is Pastor Josh. *"And the peace of God, which surpasses all understanding, will guard your heart and your thoughts in Christ Jesus..."*

"I don't understand," she whispers.

*"**Your spirit does**,"* a distinct, inner voice conveys.

Peace? Peace doesn't exist in hell.

Rahab's world becomes red. As red as the blood that spattered against her face. Red like the colors of the sunset that kissed the lake. Red like the roses placed on top of Richard's casket as it was lowered into the grave. Red like the stained tools Puah used to abort the baby. Father unknown. Red like the devil, who laughed in her face whenever she found peace.

Red was death, it dwelt amongst good and bad together. *Heaven and hell is on earth.*

SOUNDVIEW

LIFE AFTER DEATH

After Richard's death, a dark cloud hovered over the family. Hard times progressed on that cloud leading into worse times, and everyone fell apart. Beginning with Mags. She submitted to the *seven demons and infirmities* consuming her mind.

Mags struggled with holding back evil spirits as far as she could remember. As a child, they violently threw her to the ground in convulsions and attacks. The Grandmother, the Voodoo priestess, held seances to speak with the tormenting spirits. She cast them away using spells and potions. Mags was labeled a bad seed just like her father, The Grandmother's son, Cyrus.

It appeared that Mags' bout with the infirmities was over until her time spent in prison. Her demons resurfaced, multiplying and becoming more dominant during periods of heavy drinking and medicating. If

Silas hadn't come up from the basement that dreaded morning, Mags would have killed herself.

When Silas noticed the opened front door, he assumed Mags and Richard were back from their Christmas party. He headed upstairs to warn Rahab and Jayson. On his way up he heard the gunshot and began running. The first thing he saw was Mags sobbing over Richard's defaced dead body. In an instant, her fluttering emotions switched from grief-stricken to suicidal. She attempted to grab the revolver dropped inches from the corpse. Sensing her attempted plot, Silas quickly kicked the gun across the floor, then tackled her as she scrambled to retrieve it. He yelled several times to Rahab to call the police, but she stood paralyzed with blood speckled on her face and gown, mumbling her schoolyard chant.

It was Lydia, following Silas up the stairs after hearing the gunshot, who placed the call to the police. When Rahab finally acknowledged Silas' struggle with Mags, she calmly walked over to the smoking pistol, picked it up, and tossed it out of her bedroom window. Mags began snarling and growling like an angry dog. She lunged after them, scratching and biting as they escaped the room.

It took three officers to harness Mags down in the ambulance. All of Strivers' Row came out that early Sunday morning, December 23, 1984, to witness the fall of the Owens' dynasty. Mags was immediately placed in an asylum. She was unable to attend the funeral of the man who captured her heart on a tatty old road in Baton Rouge.

Rahab fell into a depression similar to her mother's fifteen years prior. She disconnected herself from everyone and everything, including Jayson. The things she loved became the things she hated the most. Her final memory of Richard, smiling and waltzing her around her room, became a recurring nightmare. Rahab couldn't determine if she loved or hated the memory. All she knew was, she missed her grandfather.

No longer could she find joy in the sound of music and the movement of dance.

With much regret after Christmas recess, Puah transferred Rahab, at her request, out of the gifted program at LaGuardia into a local high school. There she wouldn't encounter the daily pain of seeing Jayson and partaking in music and dance classes.

Naturally, Jayson took it hard. He insisted upon seeing Rahab when she stopped answering his calls. The family lied saying she was sick at first, but when she didn't return to school, Jayson showed up at the front door. The circumstances of Richard's death were already being run through the rumor mill around the neighborhood, so they revealed that the family had in fact experienced the loss and Rahab took it especially hard because she witnessed it. Before leaving, Jayson snuck around to the back of the house to see if he could steal a glimpse of her. His heart broke watching Rahab rock from side to side through her bedroom window. He climbed the sturdy winding tree and pulled open the unlocked window. Determined to hold her, he'd take the backlash.

"Rah, what's going on with you?" Rahab hadn't acknowledged his presence. She didn't even flinch when he came through the window. "Whatever it is, please know that I love you. You know that right?" he shyly asked on bended knee. She continued her rocking. "Look, I brought your Christmas gift."

Jayson pulled a box, unevenly wrapped in Christmas paper, from his coat pocket and teasingly waved it across Rahab's blind eyes. She was happy a month ago when he revealed he bought her something, but on that day, she didn't even crack a smile. Her eyes were vacant. Frustrated, Jayson quickly unwrapped the present and tossed the crumpled paper aside. He smiled brightly, holding a thin 14 karat gold rope chain with a gold-plated 45rmp adapter medallion dangling from it to her face. She expressed no interest in the gift he worked two gigs to buy. He sighed and stood then gently brushed her hair to the side and placed the chain around her neck. His heart was heavy.

"I promise to love you forever," he whispered, leaning toward her ear and gently kissing her cheek. Tears ran freely from his eyes. He instinctively knew they were over. The black *Romeo and Juliet* were dead. Jayson exited the room through the door, not feeling like climbing down the tree.

Rahab acknowledged his presence when she felt his warm kiss on her skin. When he left the room, she clutched the medallion and held it close to her heart. She wanted to cry, but tears couldn't form. She wanted to speak, but her words were lost. She continued to rock and stare, fixated on a place past reality and just before the spiritual realm. The place where *present* esteems to meet *eternal* and pain longs for peace.

Rahab isolated herself to her bedroom. Unable to conceal her unbalanced emotions and thoughts that implied everyone knew her dreadful secret, she stopped attending school and wouldn't talk to anyone, including

Lydia. She was eventually hospitalized for malnutrition and refusal to eat. When she started vomiting, Puah knew it was the *Fontaine Fiasco* all over again.

The hospital blood work came back positive, and Puah did what she felt Lotti should have done fifteen years prior. She ended the cursed life of the child growing inside of her daughter.

With trembling hands and a heavy heart but no remorse, Puah pulled out the tiny fetus, her brother or grandson, and dropped him in a bucket to flush later. She took her time identifying the body parts to make sure no pieces were left behind. Puah glanced up at Rahab's stone face to check on her well-being. Her empty eyes had turned black and sent a chill up Puah's spine that charged a memory she'd never forget. Instantly, she cried the tears her daughter couldn't produce and proceeded to clean up. She made sure everything was done with the same perfection Lotti used.

What snapped Rahab from depression was the birth of Silas and Lydia's baby girl, Krystal Skyy Williams. When Lydia returned from the hospital, she marched into the room they shared and placed the newborn, swaddled in a pink hospital blanket, on Rahab's chest.

"Jú promised dat jú would be here for me, mang. No matter what," Lydia expressed, overwhelmed with emotion and longing for her bestie. "What happened is over. It's a thing of the past. Historia! Me adiós," she continued, waving her hand in the air gesturing bye-bye.

Rahab, resting on a makeshift bed on the floor in Mr. Jenkins' guest bedroom, gently sat up, holding the squirming baby in one arm against her chest. Lydia squatted down beside them and took Rahab's free hand into hers. Lydia's eyes were red, and her cheeks flushed, but Rahab thought she and the baby were the most beautiful people she'd seen in a long time.

"We are strong together, not apart," Lydia declared, choking up. "I need you. I can't do this without you. Because I don't know about that brother of yours!" She exclaimed, trying to laugh instead of cry. "He's crazy, a terrible *novio*. Horrible boyfriend. But! I love him." They laughed at the notion of Silas being a boyfriend and a father.

At the sound of laughter, the family entered the room. Rahab immediately started speaking again; there was much to share with the new bundle, and she found solace in cuddling and coddling her niece.

MRS. JENKINS

Puah surprised even herself, displaying incredible inner strength, wisdom, and peace throughout the family's bereavement and Rahab's ordeal. She managed to get her daughter through the awful hospital *rape kit* administration, police interrogations, nightmares, and abortion. The family had to undergo a tedious investigation into Richard's death before it was ruled a suicide. There was also an *Internal Revenue Service* criminal investigation that suddenly surfaced.

Due to tax evasion and unjustified income throughout the years, the government put a lien on everything Mags and Richard owned, and padlocked their house. If Mags weren't legally and medically documented as insane, she would've endured federal prison. Instead, she moved from private care to a city-owned institution.

The family, consisting of one adult, three adolescents, one child, and an infant, all moved into

Mr. Jenkins' two-bedroom apartment in the Soundview section of the Bronx. That's where Puah felt safe to have her meltdown.

Disaster met her at every corner. Her spiritualist couldn't even bring good news. So, Puah took to Mr. Jenkins bedroom and nursed bottles of peach brandy, releasing the alcoholic scratching within. She hadn't held a real job in six months. She presumed after performing Rahab's abortion that she found her second calling. So, out of desperation and the effects of alcohol, Puah briefly took on the Auguste family's line of business and, for less than the local clinics, secretly helped women abort unwanted pregnancies in the privacy of Mr. Jenkins' kitchen.

At first, she considered it easy money, something she could do with her eyes closed. But the fetus's spirits attached themselves to her. She took every abortion personally and grew sadder and sadder. Drinking deadened her reality that she was a failure as well as a murderer. Her only peace was found in Mr. Jenkins' companionship.

Mr. Jenkins was kind to her and the kids. He offered them shelter and provisions. The only payment he required was Puah's love. From the moment he spotted her standing in front of Bronx Cedar Hospital flagging his cab, he knew she was the one. Instantly, "Brickhouse" *by The Commodores* played in his mind. She was a tall drink of water, dipped in caramel, slender, and proper in stature. Puah immediately engaged him in conversation, something she wasn't frequent in doing. His kind eyes and hearty laughter softened her heart. Feeling sympathy for her, drenched in lust, Mr. Jenkins offered to be at her beck and call.

"Marry me, Pu; I promise I'll take care of you," he asked on bended knee before they moved into his apartment. Placing his mother's small diamond ring on her finger, he promised, "You'll never have to worry about nothing, sweet thang. Please, Pu. I know I don't make the money you're accustomed to, but I have a job,

Veteran's Benefits, Social Security, healthcare. It would all belong to Mrs. Jenkins. Can that be you? I don't wanna see you lost in this city, worried, or sad. I love you. I can make you happy," Mr. Jenkins stated, adamant and confident. Two qualities Puah found attractive.

"Yes! Yes, I will," she responded in a *what the heck* kind of manner.

What do I have to lose?

She was with Minton for nearly fourteen years, and he refused to give her his precious mother's name, *Mrs. Williams.* Then, she stumbled upon a man who would give her his mother's name and anything else he possessed. Mr. Jenkins breezed in and helped Puah get her life back on track.

By the end of that horrid year, the family's situation was pretty stable. Rahab and Lydia returned to high school in the fall while Puah watched the baby. Gomer entered junior high and Silas did his own thing. He never begged for money. He brought food into the house and clothed his family. No one asked questions, mostly because they knew the answer and didn't want to hear it out loud. Nevertheless, bad times rolled in like a storm and commenced to wiping out the good.

One night, while letting out a passenger, a man jumped into Mr. Jenkins' cab as he was pulling away and held him up at gunpoint. Mr. Jenkins refused to hand over his money. He rationalized talking the situation through. The man, desperate and high on drugs, attempted to take his cash box. As they struggled, the gun went off leaving Mr. Jenkins paralyzed from the waist down.

Silas kept the family afloat in the Soundview apartment for over a year after Mr. Jenkins' injury. They were evicted from the apartment shortly following Silas' arrest and confinement on a repeater charge of drug possession. Mr. Jenkins' benefits couldn't cover rent, bills, and the needs of five additional people. Puah aimed to help. Between Mr. Jenkins' therapy appointments and babysitting her grand, she started doing abortions again. This time, she had the assistance of a new lesbian friend, a retired nurse named Shiprah.

She and Shiphrah weren't an item; they were drinking buddies. They drank heavily, dished harsh conversation, and kept each other company during the day. It was the heavy drinking that caused Puah to believe she heard the cries of the aborted babies.

"Relax, girlfriend," Shiphrah urged, comforting a woman lying on the makeshift operating table in her kitchen.

The woman's boyfriend paid in advance but wasn't *man enough* to stick around. He left their kids sitting in the living room and excused himself to go *buy milk.*

"Relax your legs, honey. Let them fall apart," Shiphrah coached, patting the woman's hand. "You ready, Pu, baby?" she asked, sensing Puah's hesitation.

Puah stood sweating by the countertop with Lotti's sterilized tools neatly placed upon a white towel in front of her. With her back turned, she took a quick shot of vodka. The young mother and the crying babies in her head were pulling at her heartstrings.

"There's no *backsies* on this option. This!" Puah said, pointing her fingers in a downward motion. "This is a permanent life decision." She walked over to the woman and looking her square in the eyes, she revealed, "My spirit is telling me you aren't ready. My cards read that I would save a life this week."

The nervous stern-faced woman propped herself up. "I tink no one ready for dis. Me man and me, we in got nuff money. In-true, we in got we house either. I haffi do dis. He gine if I don't," she related in a Bajan dialect.

"Well, Shiphrah has a pullout sofa," Puah expressed matter-of-factly to Shiphrah's surprise. "That is until you can figure things out. Because I have a feeling, lady, you don't have *a man* anymore. He's already gone."

The boyfriend had *that look* in his eyes when he handed Puah the payment. He was jittery, as expected, but when he told the kids, "Behave, I'll be back," Puah knew from experience and the money in her hand that was goodbye.

"Do you have any family, sweetheart?" Shiphrah asked, wanting an alternative to her sofa.

"Yes, ma'am, dey in Barbados. Oh, lordie, what we do? I in got muy green card yet."

Puah convinced Shiphrah to let the family stay with her for a little while. A little while turned into five months, and the lady gave birth to a healthy baby boy which she put up for adoption. As fate would have it, working as a nanny, she wound up nursing and caring for her own child until fully weaned. Moses, as her baby was lovingly called, lived in the comforts of a wealthy home. He was well educated and lacked nothing.

That was Puah and Shiphrah's final attempted abortion.

SNAP BEANS, NO SALT

*In the day of prosperity be joyful, and in the day of adversity
consider; yes, God has made the one side by side with the other...*
Ecclesiastes 7:14

"Les haricots ne sont pas salés," Puah uttered,
walking out of the cramped bedroom of the welfare
hotel apartment where they now lived.

The words floated from her mouth on their own
as though a reminder. They weren't spoken to anyone
in particular but of their declining situation. She
dimmed the room lights and took a swig from a flask-
sized bottle of *Smirnoff*, supposedly discreetly wrapped
in a brown paper bag. After saying her good nights,
Puah stood in the doorway for a few seconds longer
overlooking on what she felt her greatest
accomplishment in life - her kids. She pondered over
how she failed them and wondered if they loved her
anymore. She felt trapped between two lifetimes and
longed for who she used to be but was settling well into

who she'd become. Closing her eyes, she allowed the silence to continue beating her.

It was the hottest day of the summer, and the hotel's air conditioning unit was down. There was barely a light breeze coming through the opened barred windows, but it was better than the hot, stagnant air indoors. In the midst of the loud silence and summer heat, Mama Lotti's smiling face came to mind, and Puah remembered where she heard the phrase. She could see Lotti clapping her hands and tapping her heavy foot on a rickety wooden floor. Her head was bopping as she sang *les haricots sont pas salés*.

"Les haricots ne sont pas salés. You ever hear Mama say that, Rah?" Puah asked, returning from the distant memory.

"I can't recall," Rahab answered, struggling to recollect her French. "Les haricots are beans, right? What does it mean?" She was laying on top of the bed sheets with Gomer by her side.

Gomer acquired the majority of the mattress. Throughout the years she'd gained a substantial amount of weight. Puah shrugged it off as nervous eating. Whatever it was, it was taking its toll on Gomer's body and attitude. At thirteen, she wasn't Princess Go-Go anymore. The family called her *Big Meany*. An angry mien regularly drawn on her face. Her words, harsh and cynical, burnt like fire. It's surprising Gomer manages to keep the one friend she has. Hosea, obviously patient, is a geeky teenage boy. He looks past Gomer's front of anger, overeating, and obnoxious behavior and communicates with her loving spirit.

"The snap beans aren't salty," Puah laughed, remembering the meaning of the Creole concept. "It's an old expression, like a metaphor for *trying times*. You know how you season the beans with salted meat?"

"Yeah."

"Well, in times like we're having now, hard times, salted meat is difficult to come by. It's too expensive. So, the snap beans aren't salty," she explained, laughing again. "You probably heard it in one of Mama's old zydeco records and don't recall."

"Probably," Rahab reckoned, smirking as she stared up at the cracked yellow stained ceiling. She remembered how Lotti loved her zydeco and corn liquor. *Boy, would Big Mama be disappointed in us now.* She rolled over on her side, facing the matching stained wall.

Puah took another swig from the brown bag and closed the door.

Lotti always made the best of hard times. Rahab couldn't imagine her ever complaining about needing salt; she made do and worked hard. She used her God-given talents and skills unlike the fruit of her loins. *'A flock of heathens,' Big Mama would say.*

To be continued...

(The walls of Jericho come tumbling down when Rahab makes a deal with the devil in attempts to save her family from poverty in the finale of the, I Am Rahab: A Novel, series.)

For more of your favorite characters subscribe to
www.authorjcmiller.com for
'Between The Scenes' (Deleted verses from the series *I Am Rahab: A Novel*).

Be sure to pre-order your copy of
I Am Rahab: A Novel - Part Three, coming soon!

Made in the
USA
Middletown, DE